between

SHORES

and

SCANDALS

between
SHORES
and
SCANDALS

JILL E. WARNER

Cover design: Madisyn Zeller, Mountain Peak Edits and Design

Published by Dove & Crown Press LLC

Layton, UT

Print ISBN: 979-8-9928404-0-7

ASIN: B0DZN798R3

To the Bickhams and the Warners:
For your unfailing support and encouragement

CHAPTER 1

Margate, Kent, England, 1888

C lara Ward's heart soared nearly as high as the distant kites in the wind above Margate's beaches. At last, she was nearly there.

Not just to her new home, but she was so close to the start of the life she'd been dreaming of ever since Grandmother Clarissa had brought her to Margate the summer she turned seven. Both her dreams and the town had grown significantly since then, but some segments were still recognizable from those long-ago memories.

As her train passed by the edge of town, she could pick out the blue door—faded with time and the elements—where Grandmother had gossiped for hours with her friends about the latest happenings in town, Clara's new brother, and their health (or lack thereof). Clara had happily immersed herself playing with sticks, shells, and whatever else she'd gathered on the beach. Those had been cheerful, carefree hours.

After Grandmother finished her visits, she and Clara would go for long walks, visit the shops or watch the entertainers.

Those had been a blissful two months that Clara never forgot. Grandmother Clarissa hadn't been able to bring Clara back herself, but she still found a way for Clara to return.

Between the small, but not insignificant, inheritance Clara got after her grandmother's death and twenty-one years of dreaming, learning, working, scrimping and saving, Clara finally—finally—had enough to buy herself both the small home they'd stayed in all those years ago and set up her own shop. She signed the deed on the house yesterday in London and boarded the next available train.

She didn't squeal with the pure excitement and joy she felt due to the other passengers, but she did squeeze her hands. What a glorious day.

As the train pulled into the station, Clara jostled with the other passengers onto the platform and found a porter for her luggage.

"Scarborough Lane, number eight," she told the man as she handed him a few extra coins to deliver her trunks to her home. She debated going with him to see they arrived safely as they contained some of her ices molds, but she trusted they would be fine sitting by the door for an hour or two until she arrived. This was a time to celebrate before diving back into work.

The solicitor Clara had worked with in purchasing her new home had also given her a list of store fronts available for rent. Even as she told herself that today was purely a day of pleasure, she pulled out the paper she'd carefully tucked into her handbag and skimmed the addresses. There was no harm in walking past them, in getting a feel for what her future customers might experience. She had to ensure that her shop had complementary attractions nearby. No one could truly enjoy ices, much less the kind of ices she intended to create, if they were next to, say, a butcher. Not that there was anything wrong with a butcher, of course. But her sentiment stood. Only the best location for her ices shop would do.

She set off down Marine Terrace, toward the heart of Margate. She turned onto a side street near Albert Terrace and weaved her way away from those hotels and buildings. As ideal as it would be with their proximity to where vacationers stayed, she could never afford a shop in one of those grand establishments. In the distance, she heard the clock tower tolling the hour. She had to go farther for something more affordable.

Eventually she slowed from her purposeful walk. This was the address of the first shop on her list. She frowned thoughtfully as she took in the dingy walls and the smudged window. Clearly this was not a well-kept store. Was that the previous renter's fault or that of the owner? She faced the street directly outside the window and imagined sitting inside, an ice in front of her on a nicely set table. For sentimentality's sake, she pretended that a man accompanied her, but he was more of a fuzzy outline—just the idea of a man rather than one in particular.

Clara shook her head, stifling the idea. No. A husband was not to be part of her future, not from lack of effort on either her part or that of previous suitors. She simply hadn't felt that certain necessary spark. Just like she wasn't getting a spark from this view. Her future clientele could do better than this location.

The next three stops were also lackluster in some aspect or another. Clara sighed and took a detour down the jetty toward the pavilion and promenade. This was only her first day. As much as she wished that she could open shop *now*, there was no true external pressure to achieve immediate results, not like she had with Marshall's School of Cookery and then her first employer after that. She needn't rush. But waiting when she was this close was near agony.

She groaned at the idea.

A gentleman passing by looked her way, so she gave him a brief, courteous nod, embarrassed that he'd noticed over the noise of the rest of the visitors circling the pavilion. She faced the water, gripping the railing. The spray from the waves crashing against the jetty was even colder than she remembered. She closed her eyes and inhaled.

Grandmother Clarissa would have squeezed Clara to her side and told her "All in good time—the Lord's time." In fact, she *had* told Clara exactly that, many, many times. She very well might have said it in this exact location.

Clara opened her eyes. "I'm trying to be patient," she murmured into the breeze coming off the ocean. "I am trying."

She slipped her hands off the iron railing and meandered back to the main street. Feeling hungry, she kept her eyes open for a restaurant or café. Her attention was rewarded when she noticed a small "Available for rent. Inquiries welcome" sign in the window of a charming little shop right on the corner. Her pulse quickened. Was this it? Was this to be her shop?

She couldn't ask for a better location—within easy walking distance of the pier and a clear view of both the beach and the chalky cliffs on the east.

Up close, the outside of the shop appeared to be in good order. She would only need to update the signage. Maybe add an awning for those who might want to eat outside.

She was getting ahead of herself. She hadn't even seen the inside, much less addressed trickier matters, such as the rental terms and rate. *Patience*, she reminded herself. Through the window, she noticed movement inside the shop. Was that the owner? Or a caretaker?

Please don't be a renter. Was it better to knock or walk right in? This was a place of business, but unoccupied. Fortunately she did not have to decide on the best course of action since the older, neatly dressed man inside noticed her and came to the door.

"May I help you... ?" He trailed off, eyes darting to her finger.

"Miss Ward," Clara answered his unspoken question. She gestured toward the window. "I was walking past and noticed the sign. Might you be the owner?"

"Indeed. Would you care to come inside?" He stepped back, gesturing her in with one hand and holding the door open with the other.

Clara nodded her thanks but didn't speak as she slowly inspected the inside. She only half-listened to the man's description of the shop's history and current features.

The space in the corner behind the counter looked large enough to fit two of her caves for premade molded ices, which would be helpful for those in a rush. There was a second room currently set up for storage, but she could add a sink and second counter for preparing more ices out of view. Shelving was more crowded than she preferred, but a skilled carpenter or two could easily remedy that.

There was room enough for five or six tables and seating without overcrowding the floor when people tried to walk.

The more she saw, the faster her heart beat. This. *This* shop was sparking.

"How much are you asking for?" Clara asked running a hand along a windowpane.

"I am willing to arrange for monthly payments, assuming there is good credit to back the venture, of course, but rent is £120 annually."

Clara pursed her lips while she rapidly calculated what she would still need to account for. She believed that was acceptable, but she'd have her solicitor double-check her numbers. "This shop is positively delightful. I am quite interested and would like my solicitor to look over the contract as soon as feasible," she told the gentleman.

"Of course. I can have the papers drafted first thing tomorrow, Miss Ward." He beamed at her, clearly pleased with her enthusiasm.

"Would you send the contract to Mr. E. Banks in London? I'll leave his direction here." She dug out a sheet of paper and pen from her handbag and scribbled down the address.

Once out on the street, Clara was hard-pressed not to immediately skip away, as if she were a girl of six or seven rather than a woman of twenty-eight. She hadn't anticipated her ideal shop practically falling in her lap like this. Her stomach grumbled, reminding her that as much as she wished to exult in her good fortune, she did require sustenance.

With practiced decorum, she walked on until she found a tea shop. It looked somewhat familiar, but Clara couldn't say if that was true familiarity or the resemblance that all such tea shops had with one another. The menu was what she was expected, so while she waited, she pulled out another paper from her handbag and began drafting a letter to her family.

They knew that she'd been working toward opening her own shop, but she had her doubts that they truly believed she was capable. Not like Michael, her younger brother. She smiled. He was very bright, seven years her junior, and Clara enjoyed hearing about his accomplishments. Usually.

What could she tell her family without sounding like she was bragging? She tapped her pencil against her pursed lips.

"Pardon, are you by chance a Miss Ward, related to the late Mrs. Goddard?"

Clara turned toward the elderly woman who had approached while she was deep in thought. "Mrs. Stephens," she said with delight as she recognized her grandmother's longtime friend. "What a surprise."

She stood and gave Mrs. Stephens a quick peck on the cheek. "It's been... a decade or more?"

Mrs. Stephens's eyes were nearly lost in the extra wrinkles that came with her smile, but even still, they radiated the joy that had enthralled Clara when she was younger. Mrs. Stephens had been a particularly spry and playful woman who hadn't minded sitting in the sand with a much younger Clara, forming moats around droopy, collapsing castles. "Nearly thirteen years, if my memory serves. Oh, but you do so look like your mother when she was your age. Tell me, how is your family doing? Have they also come to see the Isle of Thanet?"

"No," Clara said, then gestured toward her paper. "But I was just writing them to come visit."

Just thinking about her family coming to see her new home, her own shop, her *success* sent tingles of anticipation and elation through her.

"Mama, we must leave now if we are to make it on time," a woman with a strong resemblance to Mrs. Stephens approached and laid a hand on her arm.

"Rebecca, this is Mrs. Goddard's granddaughter, Miss Ward. She was just telling me her family is to come! I must keep my schedule open long enough to see Michael, dear boy." Mrs. Stephens turned toward Clara. "You will be sure to inform me if he comes. Such a bright, promising lad."

With that, she allowed her daughter to lead her out the door.

Clara returned to her letter with dimmed

enthusiasm, Mrs. Stephens's parting words echoing in her ears. Even that dear woman, who'd always had time for a younger Clara, passed her over for her brother.

Michael deserved the praise. He truly did. But his accomplishments always took precedence over anything Clara did. Was it wicked or prideful of her to wish that just once, she could have the glory?

She looked at her blank letter. From the moment he'd been born, Michael was all she heard about. Here in Margate, she'd been free of that. And here in Margate, she was determined to make a name for herself. One that would make her parents just as proud of her as they were of Michael.

She, Clara Ward, would leave people talking of her.

CHAPTER 2

The next morning, Clara carefully unpacked her favorite teapot and cups from her trunk in the kitchen before setting tea to brew. The previous tenant had left the living areas in a questionable state, with some of their belongings still scattered on various surfaces, and she didn't trust the kettle sitting on the iron stovetop. Who knew how long things had been sitting out before she moved in?

She tsked and moved to the front porch, carefully holding her tea so it wouldn't spill. This view was as captivating as she remembered, albeit with more buildings in the way. Shame, really. Why did progress and growth have to overtake the natural beauties available?

Clara blew on her tea and took a sip. A couple walking down the street kept looking her way as they spoke to each other. She could only assume that they lived nearby and were noting the home's newest resident. But the way they *stared*. A newcomer shouldn't warrant that much curiosity, not in a town where people came and went as easily as the tide.

When a passing delivery boy also gawked, Clara questioned whether something about her appearance was drawing the unusual attention. She didn't think anything was out of place. Either way, she didn't fancy staying out any longer for more uncomfortable encounters. She'd see about breakfast instead.

Before she could retreat, a man carrying a bag turned from the main road toward her front porch.

"Grocery delivery for number eight, Scarborough Lane," he declared as Clara opened her mouth to ask his intentions.

"Oh, but I didn't order—" Clara started.

The man grunted. "This 'ere's the usual delivery. My brother's a porter at the station, and 'e mentioned 'e'd delivered trunks for a lady 'ere late yesterday afternoon. That'd be you, I'm guessin'."

"Well, yes," Clara answered.

The man nodded as if that settled the matter. "As I said, this 'ere's the usual, so if you want to make any changes to the order, just let Clem at the Seaside Market and Grocer know. 'E'll take care of you."

Without thinking, she took the bag from the man when he handed it to her.

"Good day, ma'am. Tell your 'usband 'ello for me."

Clara blinked. She had no husband, but the delivery man must have been making assumptions. It *was* uncommon for a woman of her age to own a home. "Thank you," she said, deciding it wasn't worth explaining her situation to a stranger this early in the morning.

She watched him continue on, presumably to the market he'd mentioned, until she remembered that she'd been on her way to make breakfast.

Once in the kitchen, she placed the groceries on the table. While it was very thoughtful of the porter to tell his brother of her arrival, she was uncomfortable about receiving groceries without her input. Later today, she'd have to go to the market and sort out the billing deliveries. In the mean time, she'd find a more permanent home for the groceries after she did some tidying.

Cleaning up the kitchen took far less time than she'd anticipated, but it still had increased her appetite. Time to reward both her efforts and her impatient stomach with an American meal she'd learned from a New Yorker who'd come to experience Mrs. Marshall's cooking while she was there—Eggs Benedict. This was a surprisingly fast meal, but it was also a rare treat for her.

The scents of lemon and frying ham soon filled the air, and a song her grandmother had sung popped into her mind. How many times had she sat on a chair in this very room, watching her grandmother sing and finalize the meal?

Satisfaction filled Clara, and she mindlessly hummed as she gave the sauce one last stir and took it off the stove.

"As delightful as it is to wake to the smell of a home-cooked breakfast, it is customary for the cook to at least introduce themself before claiming ownership of one's kitchen," a distinctly unfamiliar—and male— voice said from the doorway behind her.

Clara shrieked and dropped her pot as she spun to face the speaker. Her foot slipped on the sauce now covering the floor, and she threw up her hands, trying to catch her balance. Instead, her head clipped the corner of the stove, and everything went black.

Throbbing in her temple was the first thing Clara noticed, followed very closely by the fact that she was leaning against a warm, broad and very comfortable chest. For a moment, she was content to lie there, until her senses returned and she realized what she was doing. She bolted upright, instantly regretting the fast motion as her head protested even more than it already was. She moaned and slumped back against the man's chest.

"Miss? Can you hear me?"

His chest rumbled as he spoke, and Clara forced herself to move away again, although much more carefully than before. She scooted away from the man, acutely aware of the fact that her morning dress was bunching most unpleasantly under her, but she did not feel up to standing at the moment. She eyed him suspiciously.

She could think of only one sort of man who would sneak up on a woman in her own home, but other than his initial appearance, this particular one hadn't actually done anything untoward. In fact, he looked rather respectable—and somewhat attractive, if she allowed herself to be honest. This was most puzzling.

"Who are you?" she asked, holding a hand to her throbbing head.

"I could ask you the same thing, seeing as you're the one intruding in my home. But I'm Ellis Archibald. I'm a doctor. You took quite the blow, and I'd like to assess you for a concussion if I have your permission."

"Your home?" Clara spoke more sharply than she intended. "Mr. Archibald, one of us is very confused about whose home this is, and I can say with absolute certainty that it is *not* me."

He raised a thick, dark eyebrow. "One of us is indeed confused, miss. We will address that *after* I take a look at your head. May I?" He gestured toward her head with a confident finality, as if it were a foregone conclusion that she would agree.

She grumbled under her breath but nodded.

His touch was far gentler than his tone had been,

which might have been surprising if she hadn't come to half lying on the man. He peered into her eyes, concentrating intently on whatever it was a doctor looked for.

She found herself studying Mr. Archibald's face to distract herself from the discomfort of having him so close to her own. Morning stubble covered his face beneath a neatly trimmed mustache. His eyes were hazel near the pupils and shifted toward a darker shade of brown on the outer edges. If she had to guess, she'd place him in his early thirties, not more than five or so years older than herself.

"You'll want to keep a cold compress on that lump, but the swelling should be minimal." He sat back, apparently satisfied with his findings. "I believe that, and the headache you must have, will be the worst of it."

Then he held out his hand. "If you are feeling up to it, we have a discussion that must happen very soon. The chairs in the parlor are better suited than the floor."

Clara narrowed her eyes. While thankful for his assistance, she wouldn't have needed it if he could remember his correct dwelling. They would address that momentarily. For now, she accepted his hand without a word and allowed him to pull her to her feet.

"If you would allow me to change," she said,

keeping her tone formal despite the blush that was fighting to surface. In all her daydreaming of the future, she'd never imagined changing with only a stranger in the home. If it weren't for the hollandaise congealing on her backside, she wouldn't have dared. "I'll join you shortly."

In her room, she locked the door, then propped a chair under the handle as an extra precaution. If Mr. Archibald had nefarious designs after all, she wouldn't be caught unaware again.

Her stomach grumbled the entire time she changed into more acceptable daywear rather than a morning gown, putting her into a worse mood than she already was. A small, reasonable inner voice cautioned her about approaching the conversation with Mr. Archibald while her temper was already on edge.

When she returned downstairs, she poked her head into the parlor, where Mr. Archibald was reading some papers as if he hadn't a care in the world. Upstart, infuriating man. She'd be willing to bet that her hollandaise sauce was still all over the floor, and she'd have to clean that up as well, since he hadn't bothered to clean up his other messes.

"As my breakfast *still* hasn't happened," she announced, "I will be making more eggs. You are welcome to join me if you so desire."

That magnanimous offer slipped off her tongue

before she had a chance to think about it. Her eye twitched at the thought of eating with him, but she really did need to get some food in her. And she did enjoy cooking for others.

Usually.

Mr. Archibald might be the exception.

While she was busy regretting her offer, he'd apparently accepted it since he was setting aside his paperwork and standing. Drat. Well, she would be a gracious hostess, despite the ridiculousness of this entire situation. The sooner she could get him out of her hair and some actual food inside her, the better.

To think, just yesterday, all of her dreams were falling into place just like, well, a dream.

She grumbled under her breath as she went to the kitchen, Mr. Archibald following her. In the doorway, she stopped and stared. There was no sign of the mess she'd left behind. A steaming kettle sat on the stovetop, and slices of bread were ready to be toasted. Even the bag of groceries had been put away. She looked over her shoulder at Mr. Archibald, who patiently gestured her back into the kitchen.

"What other surprises will this day hold?" she asked.

"Pardon?"

Clara shook her head. "Nothing. Just speaking to myself."

For the next several minutes, they awkwardly

worked around each other in setting the table, toasting the bread, and reheating the ham. As they ate in silence, Clara lamented the fact that she no longer had hollandaise sauce or lemons to make more. She doubted she would have been able to enjoy it at this point, even if she did. She couldn't think of a more uncomfortable meal she'd ever had.

Once their plates were empty and Clara had refilled her teacup, she knew they couldn't avoid talking any longer. She was reluctant to broach the topic first, since offering any sort of explanation felt like an admission of wrongdoing that *she* was completely innocent of.

Except... there was one part this morning where she could have behaved better and where she was now fed, she was willing to make amends.

"Thank you for cleaning up earlier," Clara said. She had misjudged Mr. Archibald, at least in that particular situation. He hadn't actually acted as entitled as she initially assumed when she came down to find him reading his papers.

Mr. Archibald nodded his acceptance. "And thank you for cooking." He gestured at their dishes still sitting in front of them. "It's been a while since I've had anything warm to eat in the morning."

Clara cocked her head. Whatever did he mean?

"As I mentioned earlier, I'm a doctor. My patients' needs do not keep to a more convenient schedule, so I find myself often leaving in a hurry." He leaned back, clearly at his ease here.

For the first time, Clara felt a flicker of doubt. He'd been living here for some time and was proving to be competent. Had she misremembered the address?

"Now, about our... dilemma," Mr. Archibald continued. "I have my rental agreement on the table in the parlor. We can look over it together until we are both satisfied that this is, indeed, my home?"

Clara's temper flared again. No. This was *her* home. She'd spent half the train ride from London to Margate memorizing the deed. This was number eight, Scarborough Lane. And no matter how polite Mr. Archibald was, *he* was the interloper.

CHAPTER 3

After situating themselves uncomfortably close in the parlor so they could both look over their respective documents, Clara picked up Mr. Archibald's rental agreement.

She skimmed over the legal jargon, specifically looking for the address. When she saw it, she felt as if she'd fallen through the floor. Her head swam nearly as much as it had earlier, after she'd come to.

There, in black ink, was number eight, Scarborough Lane. Stiffening her back, she read through the terms. According to this, he was a legal tenant for another two years or so. But...

She pulled her deed from her pocket and pointed out her address to Mr. Archibald. "This makes no sense. I signed the deed just yesterday. There was no mention of anyone living here."

Mr. Archibald frowned and took the deed from her limp fingers. His eyes darted back and forth as he read. "How strange... They're both signed by a Mr. E. Banks. The man should have known."

"What do we do?" Clara asked. She should have

known something wasn't right. Everything had lined up so wonderfully... as if she were destined to come to Margate, to this exact home of her fondest memories.

"Well, Miss Ward—it is Miss Ward, correct?"

Clara blushed. She hadn't realized she'd never properly introduced herself. The poor man was so patient. She'd disrupted his morning, and he never once chided her or thrown her out as he clearly had the legal right to.

"Yes—I'm sorry, yes, Miss Ward," she mumbled. She stood and began pacing across the small room. Fifteen steps across, then fifteen back. She had just as much legal right as Mr. Archibald. She couldn't afford a lengthy legal battle, not if she wanted to keep that location for her shop. But they couldn't both live here. Imagine the scandal! Her parents would be so disappointed if she sullied their name in that manner.

Clara rubbed at her forehead, her headache returning with a vengeance. "Oh, this is a disaster."

Mr. Archibald shook his head. "Not necessarily. Since I am technically your tenant now, you'll be getting my rent money and can easily find another place to reside."

Clara stopped her pacing. "Me? Why would I be the one to leave? I can just as easily evict you."

"You could," Mr. Archibald agreed. His voice was as bland as if he were commenting on the weather. "But several patients are aware this is my residence, and if I were to move, I'm afraid not all of them would receive the memo, and then we run into the possibility of someone in crisis being unable to find me in time."

Clara couldn't argue with that logic. But she couldn't leave either. She'd already written to her parents, inviting them to come visit *this* house. How mortifying would it be if she were to immediately follow that invitation with a "Disregard the last message. I don't live here after all." Her departure was simply out of the question.

"Additionally, you only arrived yesterday. I presume you haven't unpacked much, and I can arrange for your things to be taken to a hotel for the time being. No one would be the wiser."

While he spoke, Clara looked out the curtained window. The view should have brought her comfort. Instead, it drove home a horrid realization. "The usual delivery... 'Tell your husband hello for me,'" she murmured. "Those weren't meant for me. They *knew* the house was occupied by a bachelor."

She slumped and faced Mr. Archibald in defeat. "The hotel wouldn't be an answer. I was outside on the porch earlier when your deliveryman arrived. He knows I spent the night here. My reputation will be ruined."

Mr. Archibald came to her side and gently led her to the sofa. "Sit. You're pale, and we can't have you fainting and hitting your head again."

He sat next to her, keeping an arm around her back for support. "We could claim you were a patient," he suggested.

Clara shook her head. "He thought I was your wife."

"Well, then... how do you feel about being my sister, who came for a visit?"

"We look nothing alike—we know nothing about each other, and if someone were to ask questions, the charade would fall apart immediately." Clara shrugged off his arm and turned to rest her head on the high-winged arm of the sofa. The cushions jiggled as Mr. Archibald scooted away, giving her more room to recline.

She closed her eyes. She had no desire to face the world at the moment. She would have to leave Margate. She'd been here one day and already was a failure.

"My shop," she moaned. How could she have forgotten that important detail? While she hadn't officially signed anything yet, her solicitor might already have the contract sitting on his desk.

"You have a shop?" Mr. Archibald asked curiously.

Clara cracked open an eye and peeked at him. He was facing her, and rather than the judgmental look she half expected, she saw actual interest and, surprisingly, concern. That silent show of support gave her a boost of resolve. She rubbed a hand over her face and sat up again. "Yes—no. Not yet. I intended to open one and had a rental all picked out and the contract sent to Mr. Banks, but I suppose I'll have to delay signing that until we can resolve this. Oh, there are just too many things in motion already."

Mr. Archibald nodded. His brows creased while he seemed to consider what she said.

Clara wished her parents were nearby, so she might ask them for advice. They'd given her so many helpful gems over the years, but she couldn't remember the last time she'd explicitly asked. Successful, responsible women of twenty-eight should be able to manage these hiccups on their own. Not go crying to their mothers and fathers as if they were small children. She doubted that Michael still felt the need to ask for aid. Not as bright and capable as he was.

Perhaps Michael would be able to give some insight? His intellect bent more toward engineering and solving rather complex math equations, but he might see something she hadn't thought of yet. Then again, even asking Michael left her looking incapable and foolish. He wouldn't judge her that way, not intentionally, at least. But good intentions didn't change actual impressions.

Her thoughts spun in circles, filling her with a restless energy that would drive her mad unless she found something to distract herself.

"I will see about cleaning up breakfast," she announced.

Mr. Archibald made as if he were going to stand as well, but Clara shook her head. "I believe that giving ourselves some distance might be in our best interests at the moment, Mr. Archibald. We've both had rather unsettling mornings, and I, for one, would like space to recover my thoughts."

Back in the kitchen, Clara set to cleaning up and only cleaning up. The familiar actions allowed her thoughts to slow, and if she focused only on getting the job done, she wouldn't think about how her dreams had turned into a waking nightmare.

Once the dishes, pots, and pans were washed and put away—her items back into her trunk for the time being and Mr. Archibald's where she thought his belonged—she attacked scrubbing the inside of the oven beneath the stovetop. Who knew if it actually needed cleaning? But in the interest of her sanity and the assumption that this wasn't something Mr. Archibald would have time to do, even if he had considered the necessity, she scrubbed anyway.

Once the oven was cleaned to a point that she couldn't find even the smallest excuse to keep working, she sat back, stretching the back muscles that protested the prolonged cramped position.

"Miss Ward?" Mr. Archibald knocked on the doorframe of the kitchen. "Might I have a couple minutes?"

"I suppose," she said, wincing as her knees cracked when she stood. How long had she been scrubbing?

As they walked back to the parlor, Clara wiped at the water stains on the front of her dress, then crossed her arms over the spot. She really should have worn an apron while she cleaned, but she'd been too agitated to plan ahead. Now she would have to speak to Mr. Archibald again, looking as ruffled as a chicken on a blustery day. She didn't typically consider herself a vain woman, but looking put-together helped her feel more in control, and nothing about any of her interactions thus far with her unexpected houseguest made her feel at all in control.

"I've been thinking over our respective situations, Miss Ward," Mr. Archibald said once they'd settled—this time as far across the room from each other as Clara could manage. "Am I correct in assuming that you have no marital prospects at this time, given that you've bought a home and a shop on your own?"

Clara internally winced at his succinct analysis. She disliked the implication that she was unmarriageable. But Mr. Archibald had no way of knowing if that was through a lack of unsuitability on her part or an active choice of her own.

Unfortunately, even if she had a man to consider hers, not many men were willing to allow their wives or fiancées to operate, much less own, a business on their own, regardless of what the Married Women's Property Act allowed. A woman's place was in the home. She'd heard that over and over again. And she did want both a husband and a home. But she also wanted to make something of herself that wasn't hidden away.

"That is correct," she said shortly. She wouldn't give him more information about her personal affairs than strictly necessary.

Mr. Archibald hmmed and drummed his fingers against the arm of his chair. He crossed, then uncrossed his leg over a knee. His distinct fidgetiness was concerning. What was going through that man's mind?

He must have come to a decision, since he planted both feet firmly on the floor and leaned toward her, elbows on his knees. "It's apparent that both of us would prefer to remain in Margate for the sake of our careers. And yet we both have reasons for remaining in this particular house, not least of which is your reputation. So..." He paused and took a breath.

Clara's stomach clenched. Here it was—whatever made him this uncomfortable was surely going to be something disagreeable.

"What if we leaned into the deliveryman's assumption and actually were married?"

Clara gaped at him. This was far worse than

whatever solution she might have thought he was brainstorming.

"Are... are you in jest?" she finally managed to get out. A weight had settled in her middle. She hardly knew the man, and a marriage between them might be a worse situation than leaving Margate.

"Not at all. I frequently leave Margate for short periods of time, so we very easily could have met and courted during those trips and then gotten married during my last one. Then you had some personal matters you needed to attend to, so I came back to wait for your arrival." He clasped his hands in front of him, his top thumb tapping the other.

He made it sound so simple. And yet it couldn't be. Who would believe such a nonsensical story? He hardly seemed the type to be swept away by any emotion, much less the more passionate, romantic ones. *She* wouldn't be swayed in such a thoughtless manner, so how could they pretend that was the case?

"Are we to live together, then, pretending to all the world that we—that you and I—?" She didn't know how to finish her indelicate statement. She refused to live with a man whom she wasn't married to. Even if everyone believed their farce, she would know the truth.

Mr. Archibald raised an eyebrow. "Who said we would pretend?"

"But—we couldn't have a church wedding

without everyone knowing. That is not something that can be kept secret from an entire town." Clara stood. She was clearly in the presence of a madman. Even though it pained her, she had to pack her things and leave.

"Miss Ward." Mr. Archibald reached over, clasping her hand to stop her. "The registrar's office would give us both legitimacy and privacy. I know this is untoward, but I do believe a marriage of convenience would be the best for both of us."

His hand was warm and unfamiliar around hers, and she stared at it. At their hands joined together. A sign of what was to come?

A deep longing filled her. Once upon a time, she had so wished to be married, to be loved, but after her failed courtships, she'd stifled that desire. Nothing she did could force a love match. It was only a wish and nothing more. It was better if it stayed buried where it belonged.

"Please." Mr. Archibald's voice was soft, entreating. "Give me two days to court you before you make a final decision. It will take me at least that long to find a new situation either way."

"But what will we do in the meantime? How often do you get deliveries?" She wouldn't let old dreams distract her from current ones. She had to salvage her reputation. But this far-fetched, harebrained scheme...

Mr. Archibald shrugged. "I'll talk to Clem, and

we can stop those for the time being. As for the sleeping arrangements, I'd stay in my consulting room, but it's pathetically small and would only invite more questions. Last night seemed to work well enough, given that I had no idea you were here until I came down the stairs."

She bit her bottom lip. There wasn't time to think of a better option, even if her panic allowed her to think clearly. She had only imagined marrying for love. But a marriage of convenience could at least allow her to save her shop and her reputation. She'd already traded the one dream for the other, so what would marrying Mr. Archibald change?

Still staring at their clasped hands, Clara nodded her acceptance. "Two days, Mr. Archibald."

CHAPTER 4

M uch later that afternoon, Clara found herself walking arm in arm with Mr. Archibald—Ellis, as he insisted that she call him such—down Marine Terrace toward the Hall By The Sea. She could hardly believe herself. She should be wading in the tide pools, exploring nooks and crannies of the cliffs, organizing her new home. Not... this.

Yet here she was.

After their agreement that morning, Mr. Archibald left to see to some patients, and Clara hid in her room the remainder of the day. She couldn't think of a more feasible solution than considering Mr. Archibald's proposal, as unromantic as it was. Even if she took out a notice in the paper to defend her reputation, it sounded absurd.

To whomever may have seen a woman early on the morning of the twenty-fourth of April at number eight, Scarborough Lane: please note that she is the newest owner and had no idea a man was already in residence, even though they share the same solicitor.

Mentally, she scoffed. Even if readers were to

believe that this was purely a lamentable lack of communication, and that nothing untoward happened in their unchaperoned night under the same roof, she still came across as a ridiculous woman, rather than the capable and talented maker of ices as she intended.

In truth, she could hardly believe it herself.

She couldn't decide if it was fortunate or not that they so happened to have picked rooms on opposite ends of the house and didn't hear the other, or that Mr. Archibald had come home late enough he'd missed her trunks in the dark. So many tiny factors should have alerted either one of them to the other's presence, but somehow didn't.

And so, rather than celebrating her good fortune over moving to Margate, Clara now had to make yet another life-changing decision in a matter of days.

Either she needed to give up on her dreams of Margate and find a different beach town to set up shop in—and consequently have to admit her folly to her family—or she marry a man she hardly knew. Logically, she knew which one was the better option. But the mere idea of being a disappointment to her family was excruciatingly unthinkable.

"They feed the animals at 4:30, so I thought we might watch that, then explore the gardens for an hour or so before we find somewhere to eat before the variety show at 7:30. If you are feeling up to it, they have dancing at 9:00," Mr. Archibald was explaining to her.

"Is there anything they don't do?" Clara absently asked, her attention focused more on the people on the street. How many of them knew Mr. Archibald? Would recognize that she wasn't someone he was usually seen with? Had seen *her* on his—her—*their*—front porch?

Her stomach had to have risen to her chest, given the number of butterflies that'd recently taken up residence. She looked sidelong at Mr. Archibald while he continued speaking of the animals they might encounter at the Hall's menagerie. He really was an attractive man. His jaw was pleasantly defined, but not overly sharp, and his hair had a silky look to it that she envied. But physical attractiveness wasn't enough to ensure a good marriage.

She was inclined to believe that Mr. Archibald was a kind man, but she couldn't allow herself to make this lifechanging decision based solely on how a doctor treated a patient, even if it were outside the standard medical setting. Would he treat her well? Allow her to work in her own shop? He couldn't do anything to prevent her from owning it, but the law didn't say anything about a husband's power to limit his wife's personal activities.

As she mulled over the many different possibilities that could await her, Clara realized Mr. Archibald was no longer speaking. How long had there been silence between them? Had she missed him saying something that required a response? She looked more directly at him, but he also seemed lost in his own thoughts.

If she was truly going to consider marrying him, she was going to have to put in effort to get to know him. She took a deep, fortifying breath. She'd never considered herself as someone who had difficulty carrying a conversation, but with a very limited timeframe, she needed to make every word count.

"How long have you lived in Margate?" she asked. Mentally, she cringed. She couldn't have picked a more meaningful topic? What did it matter how long he lived here? Still, it was better than nothing, she supposed.

"Nearly four years," he said. "My sister was in a particularly delicate situation and wanted me to assist with her care."

"You helped your sister with having a baby?" Clara blurted. She shuddered at the thought of Michael being anywhere near her if she were ever in that state.

Mr. Archibald made a coughing noise that almost sounded as if he were choking. "Not at all. She has a more delicate constitution, and I simply kept an eye on her to ensure that she wouldn't grow too frail. Her midwife did the rest."

Clara wasn't sure who was blushing more between the two of them. How horridly awkward this topic was.

"That makes more sense," she said. Then, "Is it just you and your sister? What of your mother and father?"

"We have another brother, but he resides in Scotland with his wife's family. My father died when I was ten. Some condition of the heart. My mother resides in London with her aunt."

By this point, they'd reached the entrance of the Hall. Mr. Archibald released Clara's arm and paid the shilling to enter. Clara headed toward the door, but Mr. Archibald cleared his throat and pointed to the side of the building.

"We actually go this way to the grounds," he said.

"Around? Down that slope?" Clara frowned dubiously. Surely he was jesting.

Mr. Archibald gave a faint smile. "Trust me on this," he said. He led the way around to...

A magnificent set of gates to a crumbling ruin.

"Welcome to Margate Abbey." Mr. Archibald gave a courtly bow that made Clara laugh at the absurdity.

"But how?" she asked. "I don't recall ruins anywhere in Margate."

He took her hand and pulled her along. "We do have a timeline if we wish to see the feeding of the animals, Miss Ward. But yes, you're correct. There is no history of Margate Abbey, just as Lord Sanger is no lord. Both names and structure are simply part of the allure."

As they walked through the gardens of Hall by the Sea, complete with the false abbey ruins, Clara tried to take it all in. So many sculptures. And the gardens were beautifully manicured to enhance the feeling of being among ruins without detracting from the ease of walking.

"Would you care to start with the indoor or the open-air menagerie?" Mr. Archibald asked.

"I thought they had a single menagerie," Clara said. She tried to remember if she'd ever come with her grandmother. She knew it had been a dance and concert hall back then. It'd been converted from a train station that rivaled the South Eastern Railway next door. She hadn't kept up particularly well on what exact changes happened between her visit with her grandmother and today, but she vaguely remembered seeing a notice in the London papers mentioning that Lord Sanger had spared no expense in expanding and redecorating the space into one of elegance rather than commonality.

"I believe they currently have a number of birds, wolves, and bears outdoors, including a polar bear. The indoor menagerie has a larger variety of animals." Mr. Archibald wasn't looking at her as he spoke. Instead, he keenly watched those who passed by them.

Clara watched Mr. Archibald in return, trying to gauge where his interest lay. He was difficult for her to read, which should have made her uneasy. Instead, she was intrigued. He was a puzzle or a riddle she had to solve.

"I'm personally curious about the kangaroo," he offered. "My niece and nephews were most interested in the lions and tigers, so that's where we spent the majority of our time when we last visited."

She latched on to this small insight he was offering her. "Then let us find the kangaroo," she said.

She lightly held on to the crook of his elbow while he led her to the far end of the Hall's gardens, where the menagerie building was. Once inside, they found the refreshment bar to buy food for the animals.

"Be sure to keep yourself as clear of the animals as you can," the man warned them as he passed over a sack. "No matter how docile or sleepy they might seem now, they are still wild animals."

Clara swallowed back her trepidation from that dire warning. She'd be sure to stay far back.

After they'd procured their goods, Clara turned to Mr. Archibald. "Do you come here often?"

He was a quieter man and seemed very content to let idle conversation die. She hoped she didn't seem like a nuisance who couldn't keep her mouth shut. But two days was not much time to get to know anyone, much less know them well enough to stake your entire life and all your dreams on. She would get this man to speak whether he wanted to or not.

In the meantime, she needed to think of other solutions to avoid a ruinous scandal that did *not* involve tying herself to a complete stranger.

Mr. Archibald shook his head, a stray lock of hair the color of a walnut shell falling onto his forehead. "Not very often, no. Normally my days are filled with my patients, and I am content to sit with a good book or go for a long walk once my obligations are done. But my sister and her family will occasionally drop in, depending on her health. Then I find myself playing the role of dutiful brother and uncle. Although, I'd say those afternoons are less leisurely pursuits and more scrambling to prevent mass chaos." He gave Clara a twisted, wry grin, which made her insides flop more than she anticipated.

Ignoring the unfamiliar sensation, Clara trained her focus on him. "Are your niece and nephews such hooligans?"

He shook a finger at her. "It is not them I must rein in. Never doubt a younger sister's capacity to upend your sanity. Where there is a will, trust that she absolutely will find a way."

Clara laughed. "I will take your word on it. I have only a younger brother."

"Ah, brothers." Mr. Archibald nodded sagely. "A formidable foe indeed. Oh, look. There's the lion tamer. He appears to be in the middle of an exhibition. Shall we?"

"I thought you wanted to see the kangaroo?" Clara wrinkled her brow.

"Yes, but there is time still. Come, you must see this. How often have you been able to get this close with the king of the jungle? Or queen, in this particular case." He quickly strode toward the gathering that had formed to watch. Clara reluctantly followed. She'd heard enough stories about lion tamers and their vicious treatment of their animals. No need to witness that cruelty in person. Besides, what if it managed to eat the man and then came for the spectators?

Mr. Archibald had already reached the crowd. When he realized that she wasn't following with eager anticipation, he returned to her side.

"There's a larger cage at the other end with a number of less fearsome animals," he said. "We can always work our way back. Who knows? Maybe the crowd will have dispersed and with less excitement around, the lioness may be more quiescent."

"That's a kind offer." Clara nodded her gratitude.

Indeed, this cage was far more gratifying for her sensibilities, if an odd assortment of creatures.

"Who would have imagined that the monkeys could bully the other animals so?" Clara mused while one pulled yet again on the tail of a jackal that passed underneath its bar. "Or that a Pomeranian could be such a despot?"

The said animal looked like a ball of fluff compared to the sleeker, larger animals, but held no fear as she barked and nipped indiscriminately at both her puppies, who were already larger than their mother, and the pigs nearby.

"You must not have much familiarity with small dogs if that behavior shocks you so," Mr. Archibald said dryly in her ear. "It's a firm requirement of mine that all such pests must be locked away when I am consulting with a patient, else I wouldn't be able to get anything done."

Clara simply shook her head in amusement. In the time it'd taken to empty their bag of seeds and pieces of fruit, Mr. Archibald had set her as much at ease as if she were with a longtime acquaintance. He'd been considerate, witty, and very informative on the creatures they now watched.

"Speaking of pests, brace yourself," he murmured, placing a hand on the small of her back. "Mrs. Covey, what a surprise."

His hand fell away as Clara turned to see the woman he'd addressed. Her ease immediately disappeared with a rush of goosebumps along her arms, despite the warmth in the menagerie.

Mrs. Covey was none other than Rebecca, Mrs. Stephens's daughter.

CHAPTER 5

*B*reathe, Clara told herself.

Mrs. Covey had hardly paid her attention at the tea shop while she rushed Mrs. Stephens out the door, so the odds of her recognizing Clara were slim.

"Mr. Archibald, how good to see you so soon," Mrs. Covey gushed.

As close as they were standing, Clara could feel the tension in Mr. Archibald. He was as displeased with this encounter as Clara was. If only she knew why. Since Mrs. Covey was a stranger, she had to rely on his lead.

"You didn't tell us that you had a guest when we saw you yesterday afternoon. Can you imagine my surprise when I saw your young lady on your doorstep at such a vulgar hour this morning? Mama will be most unhappy to have caused you any inconvenience."

Clara's mouth was dry. She knew. Somehow, this woman, out of all the women in Margate, knew where Clara had spent the night. Knew who both of them were. And more distressingly, she would easily be able to learn the truth of Clara's identity. She clenched Mr. Archibald's arm as if he might somehow manage to whisk them away.

Mrs. Covey looked closer at Clara, delighted recognition lighting her eyes. "Miss Ward, isn't it? Mama couldn't stop talking about your family the entire way home. Indeed, if she'd known that you were staying with our dear doctor, she would have invited you both over for dinner."

"Yes, well," Clara managed to get out. "We had so little time to get reacquainted with each other's situation..."

"Most unfortunate, really. But we didn't want to keep Mr. Archibald waiting."

She really did sound apologetic, so Clara believed she didn't mean them any ill will. But still, she spoke so eagerly and so quickly that Clara had no doubt that the news of a Miss Ward staying with Mr. Archibald would be spreading within the hour. Unless she did something now, Clara's reputation would be ruined beyond repair.

No one would buy from a scandalous woman.

"My husband is a most patient man," she said, clenching Mr. Archibald's arm as fiercely as she might a life preserver on a stormy sea. She prayed that he hadn't changed his mind about them marrying.

Mr. Archibald covered Clara's hand with his own. "I would forgive Mrs. Stephens for any tardiness, especially if I'd known she was speaking with Clara."

Clara would have sighed with relief that he was playing along if it weren't for the not-insignificant part of her that was screaming at the insanity of committing herself to such a lie.

"Oh!" Mrs. Covey gasped, finally catching on to what they were saying. "Oh, you terrible man," she said, lightly slapping him on the arm with the handle of her parasol. "You never said a word. You, Miss Ward—that is, Mrs. Archibald, are forgiven since you really had no time to tell Mama. She will absolutely insist on the both of you coming to dinner. We need to hear the full story. I will leave the two of you lovebirds together, but expect us to be in touch. Have a wonderful day."

She bustled away, practically brimming with excitement. Clara stared after her, trying to wrap her head around what had just happened.

"Well, my dear," Mr. Archibald said, "it appears we must concoct a more detailed tale. But first, might I have my arm back? I'm losing feeling in it."

That night, Clara couldn't sleep. She tossed and turned long after she retired to the safety of her room. The fact that she was acutely aware of the man—her soon-to-be husband—slept under the same roof did nothing to calm her mind. He was unable to stay anywhere else since they were supposedly newlyweds without the possibility of more questions and talk. Precisely what they wished to avoid before they took the train to nearby Ramsgate and had the registrar marry them in a matter of hours.

Still, she'd propped a chair under the handle of her door. No matter what lies they told, no matter how many people they would have to convince that this was a love match so fierce that they'd forgone a more traditional wedding, she would not compromise herself any more than she already had. That man would not be allowed inside her room.

There would still be whispers, of course. Even a registrar's wedding was questionable, particularly as unannounced as theirs. But a married couple under the same roof was not nearly as scandalous as the reality of their situation.

Clara rolled over and punched her pillow back into fluffiness. Little good that it did.

Giving up, Clara found her wrapper and removed the chair. The hallway toward Mr. Archibald's—*Ellis's*—room was dark and quiet, so she tiptoed down the stairs. The third step creaked, and she froze for a moment.

Ridiculous.

This was her house. She shouldn't have to be sneaking around in it. She humphed, pulled her wrapper tighter around herself, and marched quietly into the kitchen.

By the light of the oil lantern, Clara dug out her trusted teapot and got water boiling again. If she couldn't sleep, she'd work. Working toward this home and her shop had been her sole focus, her solace, for so long that it only felt natural to turn to it for comfort again.

Once her tea was ready, Clara pulled out her worn copy of Mrs. Marshall's *Book of Ices*. It was only three years old, but the binding was worn to the point that she no longer needed to prevent pages from turning if the book were tilted upright. A couple of them were even loose enough that if she shook the book, they would probably fall out.

Over the years, she'd poured herself into this book, leaving traces of who she was and who she hoped to become with each note. In a way, this book was as much a part of her as the color of her hair or the length of her fingers. She flipped through the recipes, jotting down thoughts and ideas as they struck directly onto the pages.

She paused, tapping her pencil against the table. She needed to find reliable suppliers for both ice and produce. The sooner, the better. Maybe tomorrow afternoon if they returned from Ramsgate early enough.

"A little late to be cooking, isn't it?"

Clara jumped and dropped her pencil to the floor. "How do you *do* that?" she exclaimed, cross that Mr. Archibald had, once again, snuck up on her.

He picked up her pencil, then slid into the chair next to her and shrugged. "I'm just walking," he said. "But if it's any consolation, my sister never hears me either. Walter, our brother, thought it was the best trick ever and tried to get me to teach him."

"Your poor sister." Clara could only imagine the number of scares that two such brothers created.

Mr. Archibald laughed. "Poor Walter. Eliza learned instead and constantly snuck up on him in retaliation for all his pranks."

Clara's irritation fizzled away with his story. She sighed and closed her book.

He nudged her shoulder with his. "What are you doing in here at this hour? It must be after two."

"I couldn't sleep," Clara admitted. "I didn't mean to wake you."

He stared at her, his expression inscrutable in the flickering of the lantern's light. "You don't have to go through with this if you don't want to."

As tempting as the idea was, Clara shook her head. "It's too late for that. Mrs. Stephens is an old family friend. Even if I were to move away, my parents will hear that I lied about something so important, and then what will they think of me?"

"You wouldn't tell them the truth?"

Clara slid her teacup over from where she'd placed it on the side and took a sip, then grimaced. It'd gone cold while she worked.

Would she tell her parents the truth? *Could* she even tell them? That she'd made mistake after mistake and then panicked? That she was destroying her business before she could even start? That she was weak and needed help still?

"Mr. Archibald," she said instead.

"Ellis," he responded, his voice firm.

"Ellis," she said softly. "Why are *you* going through with this? You could have denounced me as insane, and everything would have gone back to normal for you. Why marry a perfect stranger?"

He looked away and didn't speak for a long minute.

In the dim light, with the darkness of the night surrounding them, it was easy to feel the weight of their choices pressing in. Had Clara's lack of patience doomed them to a life of regret?

"In all honesty," he finally spoke, his voice husky, "I had not intended to marry. Both Walter and Eliza are settled with children of their own, so my mother is content with those grandchildren. And with my unusual hours, I am seldom home on a consistent basis. The loneliness would be difficult for most women."

He rolled Clara's pencil between his fingers. The

air between them was thick with the words he hadn't said yet. Why he'd chosen to go against his previous decision. Clara found herself holding her breath, as if breathing would disturb his train of thought—change whether or not he would tell them to her. She found herself desperately wanting to know this man. Find reassurance that they could find contentment with each other.

Before Mrs. Covey's interruption, Clara had thought that they might actually be compatible enough to at least be friends. But one hour was not enough time to tell. She hadn't felt that spark of excitement like she had with her shop, which frightened and disappointed her. Sitting here, on the brink of marriage, she was forced to admit that she still had been dreaming of a love match, no matter how much she told herself that it wasn't in her future. Ellis's next words had the potential to crush the remainder of that hope.

"When you told me you had a shop, I thought that perhaps a marriage of... of convenience... that if we got married, it might help both of our reputations, and since we'd both be busy with our occupations, neither one of us would need to worry about neglecting the other. And we both get what we want." With his final words, he looked Clara in the eye.

Clara's heart had already sunk when he called this a marriage of convenience. She'd known that was really what this was. She simply hadn't wanted to admit it. But his logic made perfect sense, which made his words even more painful. There would be no tender sentiments between them. Why would there be any in a business arrangement? For that's what this was.

As a married man, Ellis would carry more gravitas, and his patients would be more inclined to believe his advice. And as a married woman... Well, she needn't worry about scandal following her. And they could both live in this house where they'd pinned their separate hopes and futures.

"Yes," she said, her voice soft. "We both get what we want."

CHAPTER 6

T he train swayed, the rhythmic *clack-clack* of the wheels teasing Clara with her lack of sleep. She hid a yawn, then dug around in her bag.

"Bother," she mumbled. She must have missed her pencil when she gathered her belongings to occupy herself on the train. Now how would she make notes?

"What are you looking for?" Ellis was sitting on the seat across from hers in the train compartment. Not many people were going to Ramsgate at this time of day on a Wednesday, so they were the only occupants in this car.

"My pencil." She sighed. "But I suppose I can wait until we get back home."

Ellis put a hand in his pocket, then pulled out a pen. "You can use mine."

Clara smiled and took it. "Thank you," she said, already thumbing through her cookbook for the page she'd been working on last night. She could feel Ellis watching her, which she tried to ignore. But it was as noticeable as scalded cream in an ice.

Methodically, she transferred notes to different

lists in a notebook. She was grateful that she wasn't writing anything truly important. She'd made three mistakes already, although she couldn't say if that was due to the fuzziness of her sleep-deprived mind or from the nerves of not knowing what was going through Ellis's mind. Better by far to stop thinking about anything unrelated to her ices right now.

All too soon, the train pulled into the station. Ellis waited at the door while Clara stashed away her things. He put a hand on the small of her back, helping her down the steps to the platform. That was probably for the best, given how shaky Clara felt, although she was far too aware of his touch, and *that* wasn't helping matters.

They arrived at the registrar's office much sooner than Clara anticipated. By this point, her innards were twisting into a hopeless jumble, and she hoped she didn't look as ill as she felt.

"Give me a moment to freshen up?" Clara asked Ellis, handing him her bag. She darted into the washroom and looked in the mirror. Fortunately, she wasn't green, but her eyes had bags under them, and her forehead had a small bruise, deep purple, from where she'd hit her head yesterday morning.

Was that really only yesterday?

It felt like a lifetime had passed.

She wet her hands and brushed at the wrinkles in her dress. She'd picked one of her nicer dresses—silk with a deep-sea blue underskirt, a pink overskirt and jacket. Then, she adjusted her hat, angling it to better cover her bruise. If she couldn't have a chapel wedding with all the usual excitement, she would at least feel good about how she looked.

She took a deep breath.

This was it. This was her wedding day. And it was time to face the registrar.

And Ellis.

In the hall, Ellis gave her a once-over, an appreciative gleam in his eye. "You look lovely," he said. "Are you ready?"

She wanted to say no, but she doubted she ever would be. Definitely not before the whole of Margate would be speaking of her if she kept dallying. Still, his approval made her feel a smidgen better.

The registrar was a portly man with kind, tired eyes. He undoubtedly was a beloved grandfather if Clara was any judge of character.

She expected some sort of comment from him, but beyond taking their names, ages, and other information for the form, he didn't say anything beyond, "Congratulations, Mr. and Mrs. Archibald," as he placed the document into a stack of other completed ones.

With that anticlimactic beginning, Clara and Ellis left the registrar's office.

"Well," she asked, blinking as they stepped out

into the bright street, "back to the station now? I presume you have patients you need to attend to today."

"Actually, Mrs. Archibald," Ellis said with a pleased smile and a nod in her direction, "I sent notices to all my appointments for the day that I am otherwise occupied. If you wish to return, we may, or we can find something to entertain ourselves in the relative anonymity of Ramsgate."

When had he done that? *Why* would he do that? This was a business arrangement so he could focus on his career without worrying about a wife. That was what he said only a matter of hours ago.

Clara hadn't realized she was speaking aloud until he responded.

"My reasons for marrying haven't changed," he said. "But that doesn't mean I intend to be indifferent either. I would like at least a friendship with my life's companion. Isn't that worth canceling my appointments—none of which are particularly concerning cases, I might add—for a single day?"

He was offended. She couldn't pinpoint why she thought so. His tone had been as measured and even as she'd ever heard it, and he still was smiling. But he was somehow stiffer, more aloof.

They'd been married for all of five minutes, and already she'd upset her husband. Goodness.

Her husband.

That would take some getting used to. Oddly, hearing herself referred to as Mrs. Archibald didn't have the same impact.

But first, Ellis was waiting for an answer.

"I think," she said slowly, still somewhat stunned by the fact that she was actually, completely, and entirely legally married, "I should like to get to know you without observers."

He was still tense, but he led her toward some shops. "You didn't eat much this morning, so how does a picnic on the beach sound?"

In short order, Ellis had acquired a picnic blanket, a basket, some lunchmeats, cheeses, early blueberries, a fresh loaf of bread, and some plimsolls for both of them. The sand shoes were ugly things that did not at all go with Clara's dress, but with their canvas uppers and rubber soles, they were vastly superior for venturing into the edge of the ocean than her regular shoes. He had another large, bulky item wrapped with brown paper that he carried under his arm and refused to tell Clara what it was.

Once on Ramsgate Beach, they made their way through the crowds of other beachgoers until they found a space large enough for them to spread out their blanket and picnic fare. As Clara settled onto the blanket, keeping a wary eye out for sand from her shoes, Ellis looked around.

"I think I see an unclaimed chair over there," he

said, pointing.

Clara shook her head and began pulling the lunch items from the basket. "No need. I'm already settled here, and the sand is comfortable enough. But thank you."

He nodded and sat down on the opposite corner of the blanket as her, crossing his legs at the ankles.

Apparently, he was willing to be friends, but that did not extend toward sitting next to her despite the fact that she'd left him room. What exactly was he hoping for from their marriage? Their relationship? For that matter, what did she want?

Thinking of him as her husband was so strange. For years, she'd been excited at the thought, and now, she simply didn't know what to think. She was somehow both respectable and not simply because of *how* she'd gotten married.

Rather than falling into that depressing spiral of thought again, she decided to focus on enjoying this moment. She was a newlywed, and even if their future was uncertain, she intended to marry only once. Therefore, she was going to make today a happy one, starting with enjoying the fact that her husband was resourceful enough to throw together a picnic like this at literally the last minute.

Clara held out a small bowl of early blueberries. Instead of taking the whole bowl as she intended, Ellis took one and leaned back on his elbow while he popped it in his mouth. He grimaced and swallowed. "That was a tart one," he said.

"That's unfortunate," Clara responded. "Blueberries should only be sweet and crisp."

Ellis fervently nodded his agreement and reached for another one. "You were very intent on your notes on the train. Were those the same ones you were working on earlier this morning?" he asked, before eating his blueberry. He grimaced again but still took a third one.

"Why keep eating them if they're bad?" Clara asked with a laugh. "I'm tempted to keep them from you."

Ellis half rolled over and snatched the bowl from her. "There's bound to be at least one good one. And I'm going to claim it. Now, back to the question."

He returned to his position with a smirk, then ate another blueberry. He smacked twice, pursed his lips, and regarded his prize with distrust.

Clara snorted. "You're welcome to them if they've all been sour so far. I am not willing to go through that purgatory in the hopes of a single good berry. They're just not worth the effort."

He threw a blueberry at her, which she dodged and a nearby gull claimed. "Doubter."

Clara made a face at him. "That was probably the good one, and all your noble efforts will be for nothing. And you will never know since you decided to cast your pearl before the gulls."

She gave him a saucy, self-righteous look, then began slicing the bread and roast.

"Ha. I would never waste a possible gem of a berry. I'll have you know, that particular *thing* no longer qualified as a fruit. Far too squishy and wrinkly."

She wrinkled her nose. "The worst."

Before he could throw another bad blueberry at her, Clara redirected his attention to the rest of their lunch. "Sandwich?"

"Please."

While she put together their sandwiches, Ellis kept her entertained with his running commentary on his search for a good blueberry. "Now, that one was particularly deceptive. It had the physical traits of the best of berries—unblemished skin, a satisfying firmness without becoming a rock, a deep, rich color.... But in fact, it was tasteless. Almost as bland as my cousin Spencer's conversations."

It wasn't long before Clara's sides were aching from holding back her laughter. "Are you always this ridiculous? If so, my ribs will not last long. They do not have the stamina."

Ellis made a show of pondering her question while he chewed on his sandwich. "I don't believe so," he said. "Only on... Wednesdays around... " Here, he squinted at the sun. "Noon to one-ish."

"But it's not yet noon." Clara double-checked the

position of the sun. She was fairly certain that it wasn't directly over them yet.

Ellis took another bite of his sandwich. "That's the -ish part."

While Clara groaned, a photographer with a wispy white beard approached them. "Pardon... you two look so happy with each other. Would you like a photo?"

Clara and Ellis looked at each other. He gave a small shrug. "It is a special occasion," he said.

The photographer beamed. "Excellent. Give me a moment to set up the camera."

While the man fiddled with his tripod, Ellis returned to his blueberries. Clara shook her head, bemused, then watched the photographer.

"That's an unusual camera," she commented. In addition to the regular bulky, accordioned camera he was setting up, he had a smaller one that looked like a simple box hanging from a strap off his shoulder. At least, she assumed it was a camera since she could see the glint of sunlight coming off the lens.

"Right you are, ma'am," the photographer said, his voice muffled while he hunched over to look at something. "That smaller one is an Eastman Kodak from Eastman Dry Plate and Film Company. They aren't on the market yet, but I have connections who say this is going to be the biggest revolution in photography. Managed to get my hands on one, but it arrived on this morning's train, so I haven't had time to learn how to properly use it yet. Was planning on trying it out before the afternoon crowds flood the place, but you two just have this glow, and I couldn't resist coming over."

Clara nodded, pursing her lips in consideration. As interesting as his camera connections were, she was more interested in his observations about them. About her and Ellis and their supposed glow.

"Ah-ha!" Ellis exclaimed. "Triumph at last."

Clara burst out laughing and looked at him while he flashed her an overly satisfied grin. "I told you I'd find a good one."

"Perfect." The photographer straightened. "I couldn't have posed you better myself. I'll process this real quick and come back with that photo for you."

Ellis sat up while the photographer packed up his camera and walked off to his developing hut. "I thought he was still setting up," he said, crossing his legs underneath him now.

"So did I," Clara admitted. "Do you think the photo will be any good? He seemed like he knew what he was talking about, but what photographer doesn't warn his subjects when he's ready?"

"Probably the kind who knows what he's doing. I, for one, am glad he didn't warn us. This might look more natural than a studied position." Ellis pulled the basket toward himself and took out a couple of stoppered glass bottles.

"Do you care for soda water? I found some lime-flavored ones and thought it might be nice to celebrate."

His silly mood was gone, and he was returning to the more familiar, harder-to-read Ellis. Knowing that he wasn't always so intimidating helped Clara feel more comfortable with this version of him.

Watching him as he pried open the bottles, Clara had a startling thought.

Her new husband might actually be as unsure and afraid of this marriage as she was.

Clara watched Ellis carefully the rest of that afternoon, hoping to see more signs of how he actually felt. But even when he revealed his surprise was a kite, he'd completely returned to the unflappable, logical man who'd taken care of a strange woman in his kitchen. While the rest of their time on the beach was enjoyable enough, the spark from their picnic was gone.

During the train ride home, an exhausted Clara had dosed off and woke up only when he touched her shoulder on their arrival. Once they returned to their home, Clara made them a quick meal, after which Ellis retreated to his small study, claiming he wanted to review some patient notes before his visits to them tomorrow.

Disappointed and puzzled, Clara tidied up the kitchen. She was still tired, so it might be best if she retired for the night.

She bit her lip, torn about what she should do. Their marriage was a business arrangement, so she needn't worry about Ellis having ideas that she wasn't comfortable even thinking about. But it felt wrong to just go to bed without so much as a good night to Ellis.

The door to his study was open, but his back was toward her, so Clara tapped softly on the doorframe. She licked her lips, suddenly feeling parched.

"Um," she said when Ellis turned. "I'm going to bed now."

Ellis nodded, a wrinkle in his brow. "May I escort you?" he asked.

Clara took a step back, her eyes wide in alarm. "To... my room?"

Oh dear. Maybe she was wrong about Ellis having ideas.

"Just to say good night," Ellis hastened to say. "I won't step a foot inside your door."

She wasn't sure how she felt about this. She might be sick. Or maybe it was butterflies. At the moment, she really couldn't tell the difference between them. As it was, the repercussions of the last two days and her fears for the future were crashing down on her. "I'm... I'm sorry. I can't."

Disappointment flashed in his eyes, but he gave her a gracious nod. "Of course. I hope you sleep well," he told her.

She mumbled some sort of response before fleeing to her room. As soon as she closed the door behind her, she propped her trusty chair under the handle again.

For all that she was trusting Ellis with her reputation, she couldn't find it in her to trust him so unequivocally. Two days and a silly moment over a basket of fruit was not enough time.

She laid in bed for a long time, watching her door and the chair. At one point, she thought she heard footsteps approaching, then they faded away. Ellis must have been considering their situation, maybe even wanting to say something despite her rejection earlier. A part of her did wish that she'd been brave enough to let him walk her to her door. Thanks to her hasty actions, both of them had been robbed of the chance at an actual courtship.

She couldn't be the only one wondering about the wisdom of this marriage. She prayed that neither of them would regret it.

CHAPTER 7

The next morning, Clara found a note from Ellis next to the kettle, informing her that one of his more sickly patients had taken a turn for the worse during the night, and he'd been requested as soon as possible.

Now Clara kneaded out her frustrations with her situation. Nothing fancy. Just simple dough for bread, but the repetitive motions and the burn in her forearms soothed her. She set it aside in a bowl covered with a dish towel to rise. She dusted flour off her hands on her apron, then unpacked her trunk of personal kitchen items. Her molds and packets of spices and flavorings would have to stay in the trunk for the time being until the shop was ready—she was still waiting for Mr. Banks to send her the approved contract for her to sign.

Maybe she would ask Ellis to take the trunk upstairs to her room so it wouldn't be in the way down here, but she didn't want to go back and forth fetching what she needed while she practiced. In the meantime, she hoped he wouldn't mind her rearranging where he kept his cookware and dishes, but the current configuration would drive her insane.

There were so many things they should have discussed before they'd gotten married, such as what items were particularly important that they stayed where they were or how many changes Clara was allowed to make regarding decor and whatnot in the rest of the house. Little things that a true couple would have decided together. Or at least been familiar enough with the other's preferences to have a reasonable assumption.

Odd, really. Legally, the house was hers, but she considered it his. There were traces of his existence in each of the main living areas, so much so that she was rather appalled that she'd been so oblivious.

A knock at the door interrupted her musings. She hurriedly took off her apron, stashing it between the pillows on the sofa in the parlor as she passed by.

"May I help you?" she asked the man standing at the door.

He looked confused and took a half step back. "I'm sorry... I thought this was number eight, the residence of Dr. Archibald."

Clara nodded, reminding herself to stay serene. "That is correct."

"Are you his maid?" he asked hesitantly.

"No," she said. "I'm his wife."

"I see..." he said slowly. His wrinkled brow made

it clear that he did not see at all. "Is he at home?"

Clara shook her head, ready for this man to leave. She hadn't planned on facing this situation so soon, much less by herself. The less she said now, the less she and Ellis would have to try to collaborate if his acquaintances asked the other later. "When he returns, I can give him a message."

She ended up finding paper and her pencil for him to write his message down, and while she closed the door behind him, she heard him muttering to himself, "I didn't know he had a wife. When you think you know a man..."

She rested her forehead against the doorframe. They really would have to address this very quickly. Otherwise, the talk and speculation about them were bound to get completely out of hand due to the frequently toxic combination of curiosity and ignorance.

She gave herself a little shake. She'd come to Margate to build a name as a gourmet ices expert, and she would do that regardless of what Ellis was doing with his time. She had his name to generally protect her reputation, but she would build it up on her own.

After she put her bread in the oven, she sat down with her cookbook and notes. She had sorted out what ingredients she currently had on hand, which recipes she could make with those, which ingredients she lacked, different molds she had, molds she still needed versus molds that she simply wanted.

She frowned at her lists. As easy as these tasks would be to take care of, she couldn't know what her budget actually was until she knew how much she needed to spend on adjusting and furnishing her shop for her specific needs. She'd have to make inquiries in town for trusted craftsmen. She also wanted to see about hiring a shopgirl or two to manage the register and customers while Clara was busy making her ices. She hoped that there would be enough demand that any premade stock would quickly be sold, thus necessitating Clara to be in the back more often than not.

But again, she needed to have a better idea of what the shop physically needed.

Maybe Ellis had recommendations. It would be nice to be able to have a second, more familiar opinion on the men she hired to do the work. But she didn't want to bother him. While he seemed perfectly willing to let her run her own shop, he hadn't shown much interest in what she actually planned. No sense in pestering him about that. Besides, she had planned on doing this all on her own before she even knew of his existence.

What else did she need to take care of sooner rather than later?

She did need to order at least two, maybe three cold closets. She didn't want to rely solely on daily deliveries to have ice on hand. Rushes would inevitably come soon after, and then what would she do if she ran out of ice before more arrived? Better to have an excess of cold closets to ensure she had sufficient ice.

The sound of the front door creaking, followed by footsteps, pulled her from her thoughts.

"Is that you, Ellis?" she called as she went to check on her bread in the oven. It needed another couple of minutes, so she returned to the table and saw the note from the man earlier. "Oh!" She'd completely forgotten about it.

"Are you in the kitchen?" Ellis asked, his voice muffled by the distance. Clara assumed he was still by the front parlor, but he walked in a second later.

"Smells good, whatever you're baking," he commented. He stretched his arms behind his back and groaned when something audibly popped. "Ooooh, I needed that."

"A man came by not too long ago. Less than an hour?" Clara held out the note toward Ellis. "He didn't seem overly thrilled to see me. Also, we really must let your clients and friends know I exist. It's awkward introducing myself as your wife, particularly if you aren't here to assist."

Ellis took the note, skimmed it, then sighed and crumpled it. "I imagine Mr. Drutherson wasn't too excited. He works for a particularly—mmm... shall I say, excitable?—patient of mine. She frequently finds herself with some small complaint that I must see to right away before it becomes anything dire. She has a live-in nurse with her who has confided that this patient is rather enamored with me, so her complaints are usually an excuse to see me. Of course, I couldn't live with myself if I ignored them, only to discover too late that there was a larger concern. She'll be quite put out when she learns that I am forever out of her reach. Never mind that she's nearer my mother's age than my own."

"Oh?" Clara responded, unsure what to make of this. She appreciated hearing of Ellis's devotion, but she couldn't say that she liked hearing of other women wanting to commandeer her husband for themselves. A completely ridiculous notion, since she had only just met him herself, so she shouldn't feel so possessive. But she couldn't deny that she was already annoyed by his unnamed client.

Shoving aside her irrational feelings, Clara returned to the more pressing problem. "We should write our friends and inform them of our marriage. Of course, we wouldn't give them any details, but they should know."

While she spoke, Ellis nodded absentmindedly and looked through the pantry.

"Are you even listening?" she asked, trying to keep her irritation out of her voice. She was trying to have an important conversation, but he wouldn't even look at or acknowledge what she was saying. She suspected she was failing miserably.

"Yes," he said. "I agree, we should write and send announcements to our closest acquaintances and family. I can start after I find something to eat. I also had a notice sent to the papers yesterday after we returned."

Clara blinked. "You did?" Once again, she'd made assumptions about him that were wrong. He was proving very efficient and straightforward. She needed to learn to trust him.

"Hmmm-mmm... It should be in today's columns. Just a brief comment. I tried to word it such that it stays as close to the truth as possible. I suspect we will find that much easier than trying to keep up with elaborate lies." He started slicing a small wheel of cheese that Clara wasn't aware he'd had.

By this point, Clara had to address her bread before it started to burn. After she had it out of the pan and cooling, she turned back to Ellis.

He'd finished cutting his cheese and was now craning his head, looking at her cookbook and stack of notes on the table while he ate.

"What kind of shop are you going to have?" he asked. "I've never heard specific details. It's always just been 'your shop' when you've spoken of it. But I assume it is something related to cooking?"

"Gourmet ices. I was a student of Mrs. Marshall."

This was a topic Clara was both reluctant and eager to discuss. She was proud of her aspirations, but telling Ellis in particular about them felt more vulnerable than she was comfortable with so early in their relationship.

"Ah yes, the Ice Queen of England." Ellis nodded sagely. "I don't know much about her, but I have been hearing of her more and more. She sounds like a remarkable businesswoman."

"Oh, absolutely. I've bought so much of my equipment from her: most of my ice molds, three different sizes of her ice freezers, her ice caves... I had hoped to use her as a supplier for some of the more exotic flavorings and colorings, but once I calculated how much delivery costs would be, I decided it might be best if I could find someone more local." Clara paused, aware that she was letting her enthusiasm run away with her again. Ellis probably didn't care overly much for these sorts of details. He was just being polite in his listening.

Instead, he had the same thoughtful expression when he proposed marriage.

"If you're willing, my mother could give you some advice. She and my father owned an apothecary, so she's quite familiar with finding higher-quality herbs and spices. She might not know Margate's suppliers specifically, but she could tell you who to ask."

"Your family had an apothecary?" Clara asked.

That would explain at least in part why he was interested in medicine.

Ellis nodded. His expression had morphed into something more akin to wistful. "It was my mother's family's shop. She'd grown up in that shop, so when she married my father, he decided to leave his own trade and take up shopkeeping with her. After he died, Mother ran it all on her own while taking care of the three of us children. I have fond memories of playing in the back while she discussed tonics and poultices."

Relief filled Clara. She hadn't realized exactly how much she'd been concerned about Ellis accepting her status as a shop owner. If he grew up with a shopkeeping mother, he would be more comfortable with the idea.

And maybe, with his level-headedness and penchant for coming up with solutions, she didn't have to worry about what the future would bring. She could take this one step at a time, starting with writing some letters.

Unfortunately, the most important letter was the one she didn't know where to begin.

CHAPTER 8

O ver the course of the following days, Clara and
Ellis fell into a routine. She would try to make
him a warm breakfast before he left to see his patients,
but she had a simpler fare ready if he had to leave before
she was up. Her solicitor had sent her his approval on
the contract terms for the shop, so after tidying up,
she'd go to her shop for a couple of hours to supervise
the carpenters and painters at work before returning
home to test flavors and colors from the vendors she'd
managed to find on her own.

She hadn't dared write Mrs. Archibald for advice
yet. She didn't want her first interaction with her
mother-in-law to be asking for a favor. She feared she'd
already made a poor first impression by marrying Ellis
so privately. For a similar reason, she hadn't informed
her own family yet. They knew her far too well to
fall for the excuse they'd given Ellis's friends—that
she and Ellis were so enamored with each other that
they'd eloped. Given Ellis's private nature, it was
easy to convince his acquaintances that they'd wanted
a simpler wedding, hence the lack of fanfare and

invitations.

But Clara's family knew how single-mindedly she pursued her dream of opening a shop in Margate. There hadn't been room for courtships. They would inevitably question her, and the scandal she had so narrowly avoided in Margate would be out to the very people she least wanted to know.

So she put off writing them and instead poured her full attention into preparing her shop for opening and getting used to married life.

Ellis made it easier than it could have been, given their unfamiliarity. As often as he could, he would clean up after Clara made their meals or pick up items she had ordered. Occasionally, he would bring home flowers or some interesting tidbit he'd heard that day. In the evenings, they would walk along the beaches or on the pier.

Nearly three weeks after their impromptu wedding, Clara arrived home much later in the afternoon than she usually did. The iceboxes had arrived, but they didn't fit in the space allocated for them, and Clara had spent the better part of an hour arguing with the foreman about redoing that section. Now she was looking forward to lying down before doing anything else that evening.

As she approached her front porch, she could hear children playing. Normally, she wouldn't have paid the noise any attention, but she thought it was coming from her house. In fact, as she walked up the steps, she was convinced they were inside.

She opened the door to see three children chasing each other through the door of the parlor into Ellis's study. A stately woman with gray-streaked hair followed them, cautioning them to slow down before they knocked anything over. Once she saw Clara frozen in the doorway, she turned to face her.

"Hello. Might you be Clara?" she asked, with far too much curiosity and familiarity.

Clara hesitated. Who on earth was this woman, and how did she get inside the house? "Is Ellis here?"

A younger woman and a man popped out of the parlor.

"I thought I heard the door." The younger woman stepped more directly into the hall. "We haven't seen him yet. I assume he's with a patient."

Clara was still frozen in the doorway, letting in the afternoon breeze. She was tempted to step back outside, away from these people who regarded her with a mix of curiosity and suspicion. But she couldn't very well stay out here forever.

"I'm sorry... who are all of you, and more importantly, how did you get inside?" Clara asked, forcing herself to step completely inside and shut the door behind her. She lightly touched the edge of an elegantly ornate globe that sat on a table there to hide the trembling in her fingers. What was it with this house that attracted friendly intruders?

A thud followed by wailing came from the direction of Ellis's study. The younger woman sighed. "I'll go see to the children."

Her near-silent walk reminded Clara of Ellis. Everything fell into place.

"You're his family, aren't you?" It came out more as a statement than a question. "I presume you are his mother, Mrs. Archibald? And... I'm sorry,"—she turned toward the man—"either you're his brother or married to his sister; Ellis actually hasn't told me your surname."

The man chuckled. "Not to worry. I'm Ronald Matherson, Eliza's husband. The three hooligans you'll more than likely run into are Gregory, Lizzy, and Harold."

Mrs. Archibald smiled softly. "As for how we got in, Ellis keeps a spare key behind a brick to the right of the door. We've gotten into a rather bad habit of letting ourselves in when we arrive if he doesn't answer right away. We did send a telegram to let you both know we were arriving today. It hadn't occurred to us that Ellis hadn't warned you about the spare key. I do apologize for alarming you."

Clara nodded, and removed her hat. "I see," she said, thinking frantically. "Well, I've been away most of the day so I'm afraid I had no idea you were coming. Shall we all return to the parlor and make ourselves comfortable?"

She might have said, "Make yourselves at home," but given the situation, she suspected that they felt more at home in this situation than she did. If only Ellis were here. She had no idea how to go about entertaining his family, especially given the lack of proper introductions or warning.

As if her thoughts had summoned him, Ellis walked in the door behind her.

"Hello, Clara," he said, giving her a tired smile. Then he noticed their visitors.

"Mother, Ronald. This is a pleasant surprise."

Mrs. Archibald looked rueful. "I'm afraid this was not nearly as pleasant a surprise for your beautiful wife. We thought our telegram was ample warning."

Ellis rubbed the back of his neck. "I'm afraid we both have been out all day."

The thundering of smaller feet came barreling toward them mixed with cries of "Uncle Ellis!"

Clara barely had time to move out of the way before they ran her over in their excitement to see Ellis. Her head was reeling, and a headache was starting to form from the stresses of the day. Ellis looked up from his crouched position where the two boys and a tiny girl could reach his neck, meeting her eyes.

Something shifted in his expression, and he gently pulled back from his niece and nephews. "Do you want to see something exciting?" he asked them.

"There's a stray cat who had kittens under our neighbor's porch. No one is living there right now, so if you want to go over and take a look, you wouldn't be disturbing anyone."

Mrs. Matherson had followed them and gave a playful groan while the children's clamoring grew more excited and louder. "Look what you've done now. I will have no peace until they've had their fill of kittens, which might not be until it grows dark."

"That's the point." Ellis winked at her, then glanced at Clara.

His sister followed his gaze, and her face softened with understanding.

"Out with you all." She shooed both children and her husband out the door. Ellis stood with an arm around Clara's shoulders while they trooped out the door.

Mrs. Archibald followed them. "I believe I'll take a stroll down to the jetty. I've grown stiff from the train ride down," she said.

She gave Ellis a quick kiss on his cheek and patted Clara on the arm. "We'll give you a few minutes to recover and bolster yourself. As you most likely have gathered already, we are an excitable lot, and you won't have much peace this evening or for the next couple of weeks if you're willing to have us that long. But know that we are happy to have you in the family."

Clara nodded mutely, her distress silencing her as

effectively as tension had rooted her in place.

Even after the front door closed once again, Clara couldn't find the resolve to move. She hadn't anticipated being so afraid of meeting Ellis's family. In fairness, she hadn't planned on being ambushed either.

Ellis rubbed her shoulder. "Come sit down," he told her. "You're in shock."

"Whatever are we going to tell them?" Clara blurted as he led her to the sofa. Carpetbags and a trunk sat neatly against the wall, silent witnesses to what Clara was sure would be the start of her downfall. His family would want far more details than what they'd appeased his friends with, and while Clara had grown comfortable around Ellis, she highly doubted their ability to convince houseguests that this was a love match. "They must think so poorly of me, standing there like a ninny. I should have offered them tea or biscuits for the children. What if they went upstairs and saw that we were in separate rooms? Will they believe our marriage is troubled?"

Her words were spilling out almost faster than she could speak.

Ellis pulled her in close and squeezed her to his side. "They think nothing of the sort," he said, rubbing her arm the same way he might console one of his nephews or his niece. His arm was a surprising comfort, and she was tempted to lay her head on his shoulder. They hadn't touched much in the last few weeks, she realized, so she didn't know how he would take such an intimate gesture.

"Like Mother said, they are an excitable bunch, but they mean well. They're quite used to my absences on their arrival, and I've made it clear to them in the past that I would rather they intrude than have the children kept waiting to get settled for who knows how long. So this"—he circled his hand in the air, indicating the general state of things—"is on me. The fact that they've left their belongings down here shows that they haven't gone poking around and are going to defer to *you* as mistress of the house as best as they're able."

Clara took a deep breath. She would be calm. She would be collected. Somehow, she'd make it through this surprise visit.

Ellis was now quiet, waiting for her to be ready. He was good that way. He didn't natter on with meaningless platitudes. He spoke what was on his mind, then let her process her own thoughts.

"What all do they know?" Clara asked, slipping away from him with reluctance. She didn't want to take advantage of his kindness.

"Very little," he said, moving his arm out of the way. "Only that we met recently since you'd taken ownership of the house and very quickly decided to marry by registrar, and that we hoped to celebrate at a future point with them."

Clara nodded, biting her lip. That was all truthful, but she wasn't ready to admit to practical strangers that she'd only married Ellis to prevent a scandal. She doubted she would ever be ready.

"We don't have to tell them the circumstances," Ellis said quietly, watching her. "So if you want to keep up pretenses that we married for love, you might want to move your things to my room. Eliza will need the chaise on occasion, so we would need to share the bed."

Clara looked at the floor, hiding her blush, and nodded. "I understand."

She had conflicting feelings about sharing his bed. Guilt was predominant. This was not part of their original arrangement. Yet again, though, Ellis was sacrificing his privacy and solitude for her. But if she were completely honest with herself, she did like the idea of being closer to Ellis. Maybe with the proximity, she might understand him better and find a way to repay him. As far as she could tell, he really hadn't gained anything by marrying her, and she needed to change that before resentment developed. Knowing him better was the first step.

With that thought, she came to a decision.

"I'll move my things now," she said. "Then I'll prepare the guestrooms before they come back."

CHAPTER 9

Once the bedrooms had been addressed, Clara was determined to redeem herself from that abysmal introduction to Ellis's family, so she threw herself into making dinner with fervor. She would prove to them that she was someone Ellis could have fallen madly in love with and married without hesitation.

Ironic, really, given that she was still hesitant.

But she was a graduate of Mrs. Marshall's. She was trained to cook for the most demanding aristocratic palates, if she'd been inclined to find employment with them. She could handle a single dinner.

She'd taken quick stock of what she had, then rushed off to the market for the rest of what she needed. When she returned, Mrs. Matherson and her children were still happily engrossed with enticing tiny, wobbly kittens with bits of mackerel leftover from yesterday's meal.

Now, as she laid out the table in the dining room, she could hear the children through the grating, protesting the washing up that their mother and grandmother were supervising. She smiled as she listened to their complaints. Some things never change. There had been many nights that she and Michael had protested cleaning up after a day playing outside.

She stepped back, wiping her brow, and surveyed the dishes she had prepared. Satisfaction and eager anticipation filled her. It had been some time since she'd attempted making a meal as ambitious as this. Fillets of *Herring à la Brémont* would make an excellent hors d'oeuvre, followed by *Bisque à la Grecque*, a dressed crab, poached oyster soufflé, and a three-layered torte—although that was placed in the cold box so it wouldn't melt before they were ready. If she'd had more warning, she might have prepared a nice roast or something, but this was already more formal than anyone could reasonably expect with the time constraints she was under. Even with all her doubts and insecurities about this whole situation, she couldn't be more pleased with what she'd done.

Hands settled on her shoulders, and she looked to see Ellis's face.

"You've outdone yourself, Clara. This is incredible," he whispered in her ear.

The warm glow of his praise was even better than she would have guessed. She laid one of her hands over his on her shoulder and leaned back into him, simply enjoying the moment.

Which was promptly ruined as their guests began to enter the room.

Three-year-old Harold made a face. "I don't like that," he stated.

Mr. Matherson rubbed a hand over his own face and mouthed a "Sorry" to Clara. "That was impolite," he said sternly. "Apologize to Aunt Clara now."

Aunt Clara.

She hadn't completely registered that, by marrying Ellis, she had become an aunt. That was an even stranger concept than having a husband was.

Harold mumbled something that she assumed was an apology, so she smiled at him. "I'll tell you a secret," she mock-whispered to him. "If you take enough bites, there will be a special dessert at the end."

His eyes went wide. "What kind?"

"The very best kind of dessert. The delicious kind. Do you think that would be worth suffering through this?"

He nodded very solemnly, then scrambled into his chair.

Clara had debated the wisdom of having children at the table with them, but she'd decided that since her trunk was still sitting on the floor in the kitchen, it would be better to have them join the adults. Watching Harold squirm as he tried to behave was well worth it.

After everyone started eating, Clara waited for the conversation to turn toward her relationship with

Ellis. She could tell Mrs. Matherson was holding back her curiosity each time she looked in their direction. Her children were excitedly telling Ellis all about the kittens, though, so Mrs. Matherson must have contented herself with simply watching Clara and Ellis.

During the fifth retelling of how the gray-striped kitten had attacked the laces on Lizzy's boots, Ellis caught Clara's eye and smiled with an amused tilt of his head in his sister's direction. When Clara looked, Mrs. Matherson was inching forward in her seat as if she might dive across the table to silence her children.

"I think, Gregory, that it is time to satisfy your mother's curiosity before she falls out of her chair," Ellis said as soon as the boy finished his story.

"Why would she fall out of her chair?" Lizzy, who was nearly six, asked.

Mrs. Archibald dabbed at her mouth with her napkin. "She won't, dear. Your uncle likes to tease her. But she is not the only one who is dying with curiosity—that's an expression, Lizzy. No one is actually dying."

Clara busied herself with refilling her glass, praying that they wouldn't see her nervousness.

"Tell us about yourself, Clara. Ellis has been unusually cryptic. His letter said that you own the house, and that is how you met?"

Clara nodded, swallowing back her fear. "Yes,

that's right. My grandmother and I stayed in this house when I was about Gregory's age, and I so enjoyed my time here. I made it my goal to come back as soon as I could. Once my grandmother passed and left me a small inheritance, I knew it was simply a matter of time before I bought a home in Margate. When that time finally came and this house happened to be available, I was so excited that I rushed over from London to see the house. That's when I met Ellis."

The rest of the adults' eyes were all focused on her while she spoke. Ellis gave her an encouraging nod, setting her at ease once again.

"She's being modest, but she also saved enough to open her own shop," Ellis interjected.

Mrs. Archibald looked impressed. "Is that so? What kind of shop?"

"A gourmet ices shop." Shyness wasn't a usual feeling for Clara, but the way they all looked at her made her feel as if they were envisioning something far grander than reality.

"It's a smaller shop—it will only be me and a couple of shopgirls to run the register and take orders," she rushed to say. "Nothing like Gunter's."

Ellis actually snorted. "I've seen what you make. If those aren't good enough for Gunter's, then I don't believe it's even possible to meet their standards."

"No, I meant—that is, I believe that I could work at Gunter's, but my shop won't be a Gunter's."

Clara was flustered all over again. She didn't mean to compare herself to that famous of an eatery. She simply meant that her shop wouldn't be as large as someplace like it.

"I know what you meant," Ellis said. "But I do think you're underestimating how popular it will be." He turned from her and directed his next words toward his family. "She made an ice the other day that looked just like a pair of doves. She somehow transforms a bunch of random ingredients like cream and curried apples into works of art."

If Clara hadn't already been pink, she certainly was now.

Mrs. Matherson sighed. "I do love a man who defends his wife's honor," she said with enough of a lilt in her voice for Clara to realize she was teasing Ellis. "But back to the important matters. Clara owns both your house and your heart. I must hear that story."

Clara looked at Ellis. She hadn't won his heart, so she didn't know where to spin a tale of half-truths. Once again, he came to her rescue.

"It was a whirlwind courtship. I suppose you could say that she fell straight into my arms and that was that."

Clara hid her smile as she took a sip, which she promptly choked on as Ellis looked at her and waggled an eyebrow. She didn't know that part of the face could move like that. While she coughed and sputtered, Ellis reached across the corner of the table and patted her on the back.

"You could also say that I took her breath away," he said.

Clara shook her head and swatted away his hand. "Be gone with you already." She laughed. "We both know it was my cooking that did you in."

"As well as it should have," Eliza said. "This soufflé is divine, and if Ronald wasn't already married to me, I'd be concerned about his devotion."

With that, the conversation turned away from Clara and Ellis's relationship to other topics.

A sense of contentment settled around Clara like a blanket on a chill night. This marriage might stand a chance if they could joke about their beginning like this. Like they truly had fallen in love so quickly.

That contentment lasted until everyone began to retire for the night. Then it turned into something less settled. It was far too easy for them to put on a show and act as if they were in love, but the truth was, their marriage felt more as if they were simply companions... who now needed to share a bed.

She'd already changed into her nightgown and dressing gown while Ellis took care of something downstairs, and now she was braiding her hair while she waited for him.

"You needn't look so pensive," Ellis said as he closed the door to his—their—room. "I promise you're safe."

Clara snapped out of her thoughts, realizing she had been staring into the air and missed his entrance. "I believe you," she said.

He was tense, and a muscle in his jaw ticked. He either was not looking forward to this or he truly was concerned about how Clara felt. She chose to ignore the possibility of the first option. If only there were a way she could reassure him and help him feel more at ease. Ironic that they spoke to each other every day, but about nothing that truly mattered. She didn't know what actually bothered him. It was pure guessing. For now, she resorted to humor.

"I was simply wondering if either one of us snores in their sleep," she quipped. "I'm sure the other will very quickly regret this arrangement if they are kept awake."

She was rewarded with a small upturn of the corner of his mouth. "Once again, you are safe. Walter would have made no secret of the fact if I did, and where he's remained mum on that particular topic, I feel quite confident in proclaiming my innocence."

Clara tapped her lips thoughtfully. "Michael is so much younger than me that by the time he was old enough to care, I was too old to share. So, I suppose you'll find out tonight whether I snore or not."

Ellis gave a stern shake of his head. "If it's terrible, I may banish you to sleep with Harold."

She heaved a dramatic sigh. "And I'm sure he rotates and kicks in his sleep. A horrendous punishment."

She was enjoying herself. Based on the gleam in his eye, she thought Ellis was as well. Before she could think of another questionably witty comment, she yawned.

"Oh, forgive me," she said, hiding the offending yawn with the back of her hand. "I'm more tired than I was aware." She gestured to the bed. "My parents have preferred sides of the bed to sleep on. Do you? I already feel awful about claiming a spot. I don't want to oust you more than necessary."

Ellis shook his head, the amusement fading from his expression. How disappointing.

"I'll... use the water closet while you get ready," Clara said awkwardly. She mentally berated herself as she left the bedroom to use the facilities. She should have insisted on staying in her own room, never mind what the rest of the Archibald family thought of the arrangement. There were a lot of "should-haves" about this whole mess.

When she exited from the water closet, Lizzy was waiting.

"I like you, Aunt Clara," she said matter-of-factly.

"You make good food. Uncle Ellis should keep you."

Then she brushed past Clara to use the facilities.

Clara blinked in bemusement. What an odd but adorable sentiment.

Back in the bedroom, Ellis had changed into his nightwear as well and was sitting on the edge of the bed.

"I have apparently earned the approval of your niece," Clara announced. She eyed Ellis and the bed and decided no amount of hesitating was going to change her fate. She might as well climb under the covers and get some much-needed sleep. She was Ellis's wife, after all. It was perfectly normal for a husband and wife to share a bed, even if their relationship was not typical.

Surprised, Ellis raised his eyebrows, but he quickly recovered and joined her in the bed. "What did she say?"

"That I make good food and that you should keep me."

Ellis gave a small huff of amusement. "Oh, should I?"

Clara turned on her side to face him. She hoped he would for a variety of reasons, scandal oddly being lower on the list than she would have guessed. But she couldn't tell him that.

In a rare moment of vulnerability, she tentatively asked, "Do you think the rest of your family agrees?"

Ellis propped himself up on an elbow. "They do. Mother gave me her approval after you came up here. And since Eliza isn't glaring daggers at you, you can be assured she likes you as well."

Clara nodded, her eyes tracing over his features. This late in the evening, the dark stubble of his beard was beginning to show. She hadn't considered mustaches one way or another, but his looked good on him. It wasn't sparse or overly thick. She pulled her attention away from his face and back to his words.

"Your mother approves?"

Ellis lay back down. "She does. She was impressed with your graciousness after their very unexpected arrival. She noted that you didn't speak much, but when you did, you were witty and intelligent."

Clara nodded, then rolled onto her back. She was gratified she didn't have to worry about their approval, and that, at least for now, they accepted her relationship with Ellis.

As she drifted off, she wondered what her family would think of Ellis when they met him. She was inclined to think they would wholeheartedly approve of him.

If only she knew how to tell them.

CHAPTER 10

T he house was silent when she woke up, and
Ellis was gone. She lay there, breathing in the
indescribable scent of him. Her mood dipped at the
thought that he wasn't there to greet her and bolster
her with another day around his family. After the
success of dinner and knowing that she had at least
Mrs. Archibald's approval, she felt more confident
around them, but she wasn't comfortable enough to
look forward to facing them on her own. For his sake,
though, she would soldier on.

When she finally made it downstairs, she was
surprised by murmuring coming from the parlor.
Instead of going into the kitchen like she intended, she
poked her head into the parlor.

"Good morning, Clara."

Clara smiled, pleased that Ellis was home after all.
The fact that he immediately noticed her, despite his
conversation with Eliza, wasn't particularly surprising.
He was attentive like that. It was gratifying, knowing
that he would still make the effort to watch for her,
especially as tired as he must be, given the dark circles

under his eyes and the layer of scruff.

"Good morning," she said, stepping into the room. Ellis stood, reached for her hand, then, after she took it, gently pulled her toward him. She thought he gave her hand an extra squeeze, but it was so fleeting that she couldn't say for sure.

"We were just discussing taking the children to the beach after breakfast," Eliza told Clara, her eyes bright as she watched the two of them. "Ellis wasn't sure if you had plans at your shop this morning, but if you're available, we'd love for you to join us."

Clara looked at Ellis. He didn't say anything, but his eyes were hopeful. She could have melted. "I don't have anything I needed to directly supervise this morning; they usually don't expect me until later."

And so, nearly three hours after much more bustling about and noise than Clara expected, the group found themselves walking down the steep slope of Newgate Gap toward the sand. Braying noises filtered through the rest of the hubbub of the other morning beachgoers, which got louder the further down the slope they got.

Lizzy squealed and pointed. "Donkeys!"

Indeed, there was a line of donkeys and their handlers against the edge of the path.

"Iffin you want, you can pet them," a gangly boy called out. Chaos broke out as the Matherson children cheered and immediately broke free of the adults to get to the animals before the others did.

By the time Clara wove through the stream of people to the donkeys, the boy was lifting Harold onto the back of his donkey. The wide-eyed three-year-old was stiff, but his grin was contagious. Gregory scrambled into the saddle behind his brother.

Lizzy stomped her foot and pouted. "I wanted to ride Daisy."

"You can ride another one with your mother or grandmother," Mr. Matherson told her. "Otherwise, you'll have to wait your turn."

"But I'm tired of walking. My feet hurt," she whined.

"It is not your turn on Daisy, Lizzy," Mr. Matherson said even more sternly. Then he turned to the donkey handler. "Go ahead with these two."

"Are you interested in riding, Clara?" Ellis appeared from somewhere in the crowd at her shoulder.

"I'd prefer walking at the moment," she told him. In truth, she wasn't fond of the smell and didn't want to have it lingering in her clothes for the rest of the day.

Ellis nodded and moved until he was crouched next to Lizzy. Clara didn't hear what he said, but when Lizzy gave a reluctant nod, he swept her off the ground and settled her onto his shoulders. She shrieked and clenched at his hair while he stood.

At first, he walked next to Clara, but Lizzy started

complaining about how she wanted a turn riding a donkey again. Ellis gave a long-suffering sigh. "If you want a donkey ride, a donkey ride you shall have."

Then he started braying and swaying side to side.

Clara stared at him, then started laughing. He looked like a complete fool and was earning himself many concerned stares from the other beachgoers, but Lizzy was starting to smile and giggle.

Ellis winked at Clara, then took off down the sandy beach, still braying.

What a wonderful, considerate, ridiculous man. He behaved so differently with his family than when it was just the two of them.

Donkey rides were followed by playing in the water, where the children and Ellis ran from incoming waves, only to turn back as soon as the water receded. Clara was content watching him from a safer distance with Mrs. Archibald and Eliza, where they talked about everything from childhood stories to Clara's plans for her shop.

Eventually, Harold and Lizzy turned blue and started shivering, so the fun in the water came to an end. Gregory protested until he saw a Punch and Judy stand, so the children were bundled up in tatty wool blankets they'd brought.

As they settled into the sand to watch the show, little Harold surprised Clara by climbing onto her lap and snuggling up. She stroked the little ringlets that were forming in his damp hair.

Ellis had one arm braced in the sand behind her back to support her, and when she looked in his direction, he had the same relaxed, cheerful expression as he had during their wedding picnic when they laughed about finding the perfect blueberries.

Seeing that, it was far too easy imagining the two of them at some future point with a little boy of their own, enjoying the day.

If only she knew how to draw out this side of him more often. Or if he could imagine that kind of future with her as well.

Harold had fallen asleep despite the loud laughter of those watching Punch bicker with Judy over watching the baby. Clara found herself rocking him gently, which meant that she kept bumping Ellis's arm. The first time she'd done it, Ellis had looked at her with a question in his eyes, until he saw Harold. Then his expression softened, and Clara melted all over again.

She'd be able to think clearly again if he weren't so close.

The show had finished, so the crowd was dispersing back to their other activities. Gregory wanted to look for beach treasures, so Ellis agreed to go with him while the Mathersons and Mrs. Archibald decided to return to the house with Lizzy. Clara carefully passed Harold to his father, then rolled back her shoulders. While she enjoyed holding him, he was surprisingly heavy.

Ellis helped her to her feet. She was brushing sand off the back of her skirt when she heard a cheerful, "Good to see you, Doctor. And is that Mrs. Archibald next to you? How delightful!"

Clara looked up to see both Mrs. Stephens and Mrs. Covey beaming at the two of them. After an initial flash of discomfort at seeing Mrs. Covey, knowing that the last time they'd spoken, Clara had lied to her, she had to admit that she was happy to see them both. "Well, this is a pleasant surprise," she said.

"I thought I saw you from across the way," Mrs. Covey was telling Ellis. "And when Mother heard, she insisted on coming over to give you both her congratulations and scold you for being so hush about it all. She simply couldn't believe that you were able to stay quiet as you were about such a joyous change."

Meanwhile, Mrs. Stephens came over and gave Clara a hug and a kiss on the cheek. "I am so pleased for you, my dear. You couldn't have chosen a finer husband than Mr. Archibald—although, I don't know that I'll be able to forgive him for keeping quiet about it all."

She gave Ellis a playful glare with her last line.

"I do apologize," Ellis said with a gracious bow.

"I really had no intention to deceive anyone. I simply didn't know when Clara would be joining me. She had business to attend to, and we were unsure how long it would take. And you must excuse me... I promised my nephew we would search for creatures in the tide pools."

Gregory had retreated toward the water already but stopped when he realized that Ellis wasn't following him.

The women murmured their acknowledgments, and he left Clara alone with them.

"What business would keep you from joining your husband? It must have been terribly important to drag you away from him so soon after you were married." Mrs. Stephens's concern was palpable in her tone, and Clara rushed to reassure her.

"Nothing terrible at all. I simply had to finish my employment as a cook for a family in London, then discuss business matters with my solicitor." Another half-truth that left Clara with a sour taste in her mouth. How she hated lying to poor Mrs. Stephens, but there really was no helping it at this point. She couldn't very well announce that she actually hadn't met Ellis until a little over a month ago. She didn't know what the bigger scandal would be—the fact that she'd shared a roof with him while unmarried or that they lied about being married to cover up that fact.

Mrs. Covey exchanged a confused look with Mrs.

Stephens. "You had... business matters?"

"For the ices shop I'm opening. It's—" She broke off. She'd almost told them that it was the reason she'd come to Margate in the first place. "Well, no matter. I'm sure you don't want to hear all the stuffy details about the legalities and logistics of setting up."

Mrs. Stephens laid a hand on Clara's arm. "You are in earnest? You are opening a shop?"

"The grand opening is two weeks away," Clara said.

Mrs. Covey's eyes were now wide. "Goodness. However will you manage running both a shop and a household? I couldn't imagine adding another responsibility on top of children. I'm exhausted simply thinking of the possibility. You are a much hardier woman than I ever was."

Clara looked away. Until just this morning, children hadn't been anywhere near the plan for Clara. Who knew if they ever would be? She and Ellis had never broached the topic. Why would they when it was clear that theirs was purely a marriage meant to prevent scandal?

Mrs. Stephens squeezed Clara's arm. "Don't you worry one bit about caring for your children, Clara. Your sweet grandmother was a wonderful woman who taught her daughter well, and I have no doubt that her granddaughter will be equally capable, given both of their examples. In fact, I told your mother so when she told me how you all were so disappointed after that whole situation with Mr. Sternes. I said, 'Beatrice, don't you worry about Clara. Give her time to recover from her broken heart, and you'll find yourself a doting grandmother yet.' And here you are—five years later, and you've found yourself a paragon of a man. Mr. Sternes could only dream of measuring up to your Mr. Archibald."

How was it that such cheerful confidence in Clara's presumed happiness—both current and future—could bring Clara down so low? Mrs. Stephens would be horribly distressed if she knew how much her words, meant to encourage Clara, stung. It was all Clara could do to muster up a smile, nod, then bid the women goodbye.

Not only was Clara a fraud, but Mrs. Stephens had inadvertently confirmed Clara's deepest fears.

She was a disappointment to her family.

CHAPTER 11

C lara wasn't sure how she made it through the rest of the day. She'd left the beach to clean up, then once again threw herself with vigor into preparing her shop. She had two weeks to make it perfect—to prove to her family that even though she hadn't married Mr. Sternes or any of her other suitors, she could make them proud of her. That she could still do something, even if she would never be a mother.

Would the fact that she *was* married change how they viewed her shop? Would they expect her to leave it, to take up the role of housewife and mother? Mrs. Stephens had implied that was what Clara's mother most wished for.

Michael would have to fulfill that dream for her whenever he did marry.

After dinner, Clara had excused herself. She couldn't stand seeing Ellis with his niece and nephews right now. It hurt too much.

Now, in the privacy of Ellis's room, Clara took out her tangled emotions on ironing the laundry. She'd heated the iron while she'd made dinner, and after hauling in the ironing board to the bedroom, she was now making steady progress on Ellis's clothing while Mrs. Stephens's words echoed in her head.

A quiet tap on the door was the only warning she got before Ellis entered. He looked somber—no, concerned.

"We need to talk," Ellis said.

The intensity of his stare further pressed on Clara's already fragile emotions, making her heart beat uncomfortably fast.

"What about your family?" She looked back at her ironing so she didn't have to face him. They'd been married for a month already, and while Clara trusted Ellis—felt more comfortable around him than most people—they were little more than strangers.

"Mother's retiring early for the night. Eliza and Ronald are putting the children to bed."

Clara nodded but didn't respond. Instead, she laid the shirt she'd just finished on top of the laundry to be put away and pulled out the next item—one of Ellis's linen waistcoats.

"Clara." Ellis's voice was soft, entreating. "You've been out of sorts ever since we left the beach. Was it something I said? Or did?"

Clara shook her head and swallowed back the emotions that were fighting to come out. "No," she managed, but even to herself it sounded strangled.

"Something I didn't do?"

She laughed, but it came out as half sob. "No, nothing to do with you or your family."

She felt, more than saw, him come closer. How strange that she was so aware of him. She didn't think she'd ever noticed anything about anyone as much as she did about Ellis. No one had ever made her feel so... conflicted. She was both lost and safe with him.

He didn't say anything for a long moment. Then...

"I was too far away to make out much of your conversation with Mrs. Stephens and her daughter, but I did overhear something about a broken heart and a Mr. Sternes. I know neither one of us has really been open with the other, but I do want you to know that I am willing to listen to what matters to you."

Clara finally looked at him. "Thank you," she said softly. His offer meant more than she anticipated. She realized she did need to share at least a little of what was weighing on her before she collapsed like a molded ice that hadn't frozen long enough.

"My family—my mother in particular—all believed that Mr. Sternes and I were perfect together. The truth, though, is that while he and I were fond of each other, neither one of us cared about the other in that way, so we decided to go our separate ways. He married a year or so later."

Ellis made a noise of acknowledgement in his throat.

"So your heart was broken, not by a specific man but more... the lack of a man?"

Clara wrinkled her brow. She'd never considered herself that sort of woman, but she could see how her explanation was coming across that way. "No. It's more... I knew I'd disappointed my parents. We'd always talked about me getting married and moving to Margate. But when Mr. Sternes stopped coming by, those conversations stopped. It was as if my parents had given up hope."

Clara sighed. How ironic that her youthful dreams were now fulfilled, albeit in a somewhat warped manner—she *was* married and living not only in Margate but in the same house where that dream was born.

"What about your shop? How did that fit in with marriage?"

"The plan was always to come back to Margate. I didn't think of an ices shop until I heard about Mrs. Marshall's school." She traced the paisley pattern of Ellis's waistcoat lying on the ironing board.

Ellis rested his hand on the ironing board, close enough that the tips of their littlest fingers brushed against each other. Even that scant contact had Clara longing for more. If she were brave enough, she just had to move her hand less than an inch to put it within easy grasping of his. As much as she wanted to feel his strength, she wanted something more from him.

Something deeper. More meaningful. More painful if this whole sham of a marriage fell apart.

"How long ago was that?"

"Hmmm?" She looked away from their hands.

Ellis shifted, resting an elbow on the board to face her more directly. "The school?"

"Oh." Clara sighed. "How long ago was that now? Maybe four years?"

Her thoughts were becoming muddled. Just like her dreams. Ellis had a strange impact on her. Nothing had deterred her from pushing through the obstacles in her way. But Ellis... She couldn't figure him out. Was he an obstacle? A detour? Something more?

"That short? I had assumed this had been an older idea of yours."

Clara nearly snorted. She supposed that four years was a short amount of time. But even without Ellis confusing her, those days at the school felt like they were a lifetime ago. Her entire focus had been on gleaning every tiny tip she could from Mrs. Marshall. The woman hadn't been nearly as renowned then as she was now, but Clara had sensed that there was something special there. She'd hoped that maybe some of that specialness would rub off on her and that she'd finally be someone her family would be proud to speak of.

Instead of becoming Margate's version of Agnes Marshall, here she was, pathetically wishing her husband would hold her hand, rather than taking it herself. Ellis was a good man and would hold her hand all day if she asked. But did he even want to?

What if he changed his mind about their marriage and grew resentful of her? Clara would rather face all the scandal and disapproval in the world than know that Ellis was unhappy because he chose to rescue her from her folly—that Ellis was unhappy with *her*.

"Clara."

Ellis was hesitant. That alone was enough for Clara's full attention. Ellis was never hesitant. He was slow, deliberate, thoughtful. But never hesitant.

"I told you before that I hadn't planned on marriage. That's not completely accurate."

Clara was staring. She knew she was, but she couldn't look away. She felt that whatever her husband was about to say meant more to him than anything else he'd ever told her.

"I was engaged once. But I was young and still in medical school. I was determined to make something of myself—to be more than the poor apothecary boy." Ellis had found a loose thread hanging from the ironing board and was twisting it around his finger. "Suzette wanted more from me than I could give—wanted to give—at that time. After she ended things, I simply lost interest. I thought I was content with my lot, but then you came crashing into my life, and for the first time in nearly a decade, I was intrigued."

He glanced quickly at Clara before continuing. "I don't know everything that happened between you and Mr. Sternes, but I find it hard to believe that your parents ever gave up hope on you. If they were disappointed, it would have been in him. I've only known you for a handful of weeks, and even I can tell you that Mr. Sternes didn't realize what a treasure he had; otherwise, he wouldn't have ever let you go."

He leaned forward and gently kissed her forehead. "I'll be downstairs in case Eliza or Ronald decides to return."

With that, he left with Clara still gaping at him.

Her confusion was still there, but Ellis had left her with the soft, warm fluttering of hope beating inside her chest.

CHAPTER 12

A couple of days later, Clara and Mrs. Archibald had just finished cleaning up lunch when Ellis returned from another appointment.

He walked into the kitchen, and without any preamble, said, "Both of my afternoon appointments canceled. Fancy an outing?"

Clara and Mrs. Archibald exchanged bemused looks. After Ellis's confession the other night, Clara felt more secure. She still didn't know what to make of him, but the memory of him calling her a treasure made her want to squeal and hug herself tightly. She was being ridiculous, but for once, she didn't care.

"Depends on what you have in mind," Clara said. She already knew she would go along with whatever his plan was. She simply wanted to tease him a little. "I was going to stop by the print shop to get the flyers for the shop's opening."

"We can do that afterward, and I'll help you deliver them."

Clara placed a fist on her hip and stared at him. "Ellis Archibald. What do you have in mind?"

"You've heard Eliza reading the children *Alice in Wonderland*? I thought we might take them to see Margate's most famous rabbit hole."

Clara furrowed her brow. "I have not heard of Margate's rabbit hole. What is it?"

"Only some immense smuggling caves." Ellis waggled his eyebrows at Clara.

She gave him a look, fighting back a smile. "The eyebrow thing is a little much."

"What, this?" He waggled them again. "You don't like it when I do this? The children find it most amusing."

Clara didn't deign to respond to that. Instead, she turned to Mrs. Archibald. "Was he this ridiculous as a child?"

Mrs. Archibald smiled fondly. "Even more so. Near drove me to Bedlam, he did."

"I can believe that," Clara said, finally giving in to her impulse to laugh. "It's absolutely maddening. Very well, Ellis. I shall go see your rabbit hole."

An hour later, Gregory and Lizzy were pestering Ellis with questions as their group walked to Trinity Square. "Is this *really* the rabbit hole Alice fell down? Will it be dark? How many monsters live in it? Are pirates buried there?"

Harold had once again claimed Clara's hand and kept pulling her forward, only to fall behind a few seconds later, so she didn't pay much attention to

Ellis's answers despite her curiosity.

"Enough, children," Ronald finally said while Ellis paid the entrance fee of three pence a person. "Let your aunt and uncle walk together for once. You can monopolize their attention again *after* we are done touring the cave. Harold, do you want to walk with Mother or me? Gregory and Lizzy, stay close to Grandmother Archibald."

Their excited chatter increased as they entered the cave, the adults each holding a lantern for light or, in Eliza's case, holding Harold's hand.

"So," Clara said, sidling up to Ellis's side and wrapping her hand around his arm now that he was free. "Tell me about this rabbit hole of yours. How does it relate to Miss Alice's adventures?"

Ellis pulled her in closer to his side as they descended into the darkness of the cave, sending another thrill through Clara. "It doesn't. Not really, anyway. A Mr. Francis Forster owned the land around the turn of the century and kept losing rabbits, so either he or his gardener—I forget which—stumbled on a hole and discovered the caves. I believe that they were former chalk mines, but it has been quite some time since they were used as such. During Mr. Forster's tenure as owner of the Vortigern caves, someone painted some curious artwork on the walls. Now Mr. Norwood, a grocer over on Cecil Square, has ownership and takes great delight in claiming these were smugglers' caves."

"And were they?" Clara found the whole idea of the Vortigern caves fascinating. Could smugglers really have used these caves as their hideout? What was it about the paintings that made them curious?

Ellis shrugged. "Who really knows? I have my doubts since these caves are so far from the water and are in the middle of town. But I suppose it is possible."

The light from their lanterns sent eerie shadows dancing across the rough, chalky walls of the cave. Clara gasped as they approached the first of the paintings.

"This one is... a running horse?" She held her lantern closer to examine the dark image. She couldn't resist touching it, though she felt only the texture of the walls. She turned and spotted a second image. "It looks so primitive. And that is—what is that supposed to be?"

On the opposite wall was a fearsome-looking creature with a gaping mouth and sharp teeth.

Ellis frowned as he considered the painting. "A dragon? But it lacks wings. Perhaps it's meant to be a hippo."

His voice echoed off the walls, and Gregory came running back, determined to see the dragon for himself despite his mother's admonitions to stay close. Harold started crying when he noticed the creature, and Lizzy kept asking if they could explore more. Eventually, they were able to convince Gregory to move on while Mrs. Archibald took Harold and was able to soothe him with promises that there was nothing that could eat him in the cavern and that they would all have a treat afterward. The treat, of course, was Clara's idea. She had some cream she wanted to use this afternoon before it curdled, and a sweet ice would do nicely.

Tunnels branched off the main tunnel that their group walked down. The darkness made even the children speak more softly. Every now and then, they would spot another painting on the walls or walk down some steps carved into the floor. They all marveled at the dedication of the soul who made that effort.

At one point, they entered a large chamber, which appeared to have an altar at the end. The lantern light flickered off a lump of something, and Clara went to examine it. The children were getting bored and hungry, so the Mathersons and Mrs. Archibald decided to continue. Ellis stayed with Clara, keeping a hand close to her side in case she tripped over a rock or crack.

Clara couldn't make out what the lump was supposed to have been and turned away from it with disappointment only to be rewarded for her curiosity. Higher on the wall, some two feet or so above Clara's head were the giant remains of an ammonite.

"That thing must have been a beast," she said, staring awestruck at the solidified coils. "It must be two feet or more across."

She stared at it a moment longer before turning toward Ellis to continue exploring. He watched her, a faint grin on his face.

"What are you thinking?" Clara asked, cocking her head. This marriage would be inordinately easier if she knew what made her husband smile like that. If she knew what his inner thoughts were.

Ellis pursed his lips, clearly fighting back a laugh, and shook his head.

"Come, you must tell me." Clara's curiosity was piqued. Nothing about this ammonite struck her as particularly funny, so it had to be something else.

Ellis simply clamped his mouth shut and gestured grandly for her to precede him out of the chamber.

"Not until you tell me what is so amusing," Clara said, poking him in the ribs.

He flinched away from her. "Not happening," he said, trying to sound unaffected.

Clara grinned wickedly. It appeared her husband was sensitive on his side. She poked him again and was rewarded with him swatting away her hand.

She smirked. She was willing to wager her shop's success that he most definitely was ticklish in that area. A fact that she would take as much advantage of as possible.

She reached toward him, and he danced away from her fingers.

"Will you stop that, woman?" He sounded more amused rather than exasperated, so Clara decided to push her luck. What other places might reward her with a reaction? Eventually, she'd get him to tell her what he found so entertaining.

"What?" Clara asked innocently. "I thought I saw some lint on your jacket. Hold still while I get it."

She set down her lantern then lunged toward him, trying to reach his ribs on either side.

Ellis laughed, grabbed her wrists and pinned his elbows to his side, effectively trapping her. She squirmed, trying to free herself. His face was lit up with triumph, and Clara's giggles were causing her to double over, nearly pulling him to the ground with her. His chuckles sounded nearly as breathless as she felt.

"Are you ready to give up?" Ellis asked.

Clara shook her head, still giggling. She wouldn't allow him to best her this way. She lacked the strength to pull free, but she wasn't entirely helpless.

She twisted in his grip and kissed him.

His laughs abruptly cut off in his surprise, and Clara found herself grinning against his lips. She was winning now. She returned to kissing him, teasing him with feather-light brushes. Ellis's grip on her wrists loosened, so Clara turned to face him more directly, her hands brushing against his chest.

Ellis let go of her wrists entirely and wrapped his arms around her back, pulling her deeper into their kiss, capturing her more fully than before.

Her knees went weak, and she forgot all about winning.

This was the man she'd married.

Heaven help her, but she'd completely fallen in love with her husband.

He finally pulled back, allowing both of them to recover their breath. Clara rested her head against his chest, feeling his heart beating with a rapidity that matched hers. Ellis's arms were strong around her back, filling her with the deepest peace and security she'd ever known.

They stayed that way until young voices echoing through the tunnels reminded them that they were not entirely alone, no matter how isolated it seemed there in the dimly lit cave.

"I think, my dear," he whispered, "you've won this round."

"Hmm?" Clara tilted her head up, reluctant to step away from him.

He brushed his lips against her forehead. "I'd been thinking that even your silences spoke volumes. You make all sorts of sounds when you're thinking."

Clara swatted at him while he chuckled again and stepped away, just as another light began to fill their section of the cave.

"I told you that you wouldn't want to know," he whispered to her as he picked up their lantern from where she'd left it.

Clara pursed her lips, determined to stay silent. She'd take that embarrassing little tidbit in exchange for a kiss like the one they'd shared.

CHAPTER 13

Somehow Clara and Ellis found their way out of the caves with only a few more kisses stolen behind his family's backs. Holding his hand, she felt shy and snuck glances at him, only to see him sneaking as many looks at her. If this is what a love match felt like, Clara could go the rest of her life living only off the spurts of pure emotion currently flooding her. Who knew that a person could feel so *intensely*? She couldn't name whatever this was, so calling it love had to suffice.

Unfortunately, responsibilities demanded that she return to earth from the clouds of bliss. She still had to retrieve her flyers and see about placing them in some of the various shops around Margate before her shop opened. After reassuring Harold, Lizzy, and Gregory that she would return as quickly as she could to make them ices, she and Ellis hurried off.

Due to his assistance and familiarity with both Margate and the local shopkeepers, their errand took them only a couple of hours. It would have taken Clara most of the afternoon, and she seriously doubted she would have been able to place as many flyers as she did with Ellis's help.

On their way home, they passed Mrs. Covey and her husband walking on the other side of the street. The friendly matron gave them a cheery wave while her husband contented himself with a grave nod.

"Those two are the most mismatched couple I've ever met," Ellis commented. "She has no sense of social conventions and will immediately claim a new acquaintance as an intimate friend and chatter all day if you let her, while he's possibly the biggest grump in town. And yet I believe they're more devoted to each other than anyone else I've had the pleasure to meet."

Clara nodded, wrapping her hand more firmly around his arm. She hoped that one day, someone might say that about her and Ellis—the bit about devotion, at least. She was inclined to believe that they were better matched than the Coveys, even if she hadn't met Mr. Covey yet. He really did look dour.

Before they took two steps, they heard Mrs. Covey calling to them.

"My dear Archibalds! I simply *must* ask you something."

They turned while she scurried across the street, dragging her husband with her.

Clara tried to suppress her amused smile, but seeing Ellis attempt the same thing made the task that much harder. Fortunately, she managed to regain control before the Coveys reached them.

Mrs. Covey flapped one hand at them while the other rested on her chest as she tried to regain her breath. Whether her breathlessness was a result of her haste or her excitement, Clara really couldn't say.

"Oh, you two are so delightfully in love." She sighed. "Seeing you together reminds me of when my Mr. Covey and I were blissful newlyweds. We weren't living in Margate then, you understand, but had a set of rooms above a clerk's office in Portsmouth—"

Mr. Covey coughed. "They'd prefer you get on with it." He grunted.

Clara regretted that she had to agree with his sentiment, at least this afternoon. If she hadn't promised the Matherson children ices, she would have happily listened to Mrs. Covey's stories.

Mrs. Covey tutted. "Nonsense. There's nothing wrong with a little chitchat before getting to business."

Turning back to Ellis and Clara, she rested a hand on Mr. Covey's arm. "Forgive him," she said. "He always gets testy when our afternoon amble is interrupted. But now that we're here, I might as well get on with it. I wanted to ask you both, together, about a date for having you over for dinner. Mr. Covey has business he must see to in Wales of all places, but he is eager to get to know our Mrs. Archibald and has agreed to postpone until after our dinner if it's at all possible."

"Eager is overdoing it," the man in question grumbled.

At least, that's what Clara believed he said. His voice was quite deep and some agitated gulls nearby made hearing anything difficult.

"Hush, you. Always teasing me." Mrs. Covey cheerfully shook her head at her husband.

Clara doubted he was actually jesting until she caught a mischievous gleam in his eye. She glanced at Ellis, who stood back, observing. He gave her a subtle smirk, letting her know that he, too, had seen it.

Even if Clara hadn't already been enticed by the idea of spending time with her beloved Mrs. Stephens and the gregarious Mrs. Covey, she was intrigued by the relationship between both Coveys.

"We would be delighted," Clara said warmly. "Mr. Archibald's family is visiting for another week, but we will be available after their departure."

Mrs. Covey gave an excited little bounce, completely at odds with her matronly appearance. "Splendid. Mother will be so pleased to see you both. Mr. Covey does not at all begrudge delaying his trip that long. Time with family is so precious and goes by so quickly."

She drew another breath as if she had more to say, so Ellis quickly interjected. "That is very kind of you both. We would love to visit longer, but we must be going. Clara promised ices to my niece and nephews. Give Mrs. Stephens our best wishes. I shall send a note later, and we can arrange the specifics. Good afternoon."

Mr. Covey nodded farewell to them both and took his wife by the shoulders to steer her away.

"Until then, my lovelies," Mrs. Covey chirped over her shoulder.

Ellis waited until they had walked some distance away from the Coveys before giving Clara a droll look.

"Besotted."

That singular word finally did in Clara's restraint. The laughter she'd been holding back tumbled free, mixing with his softer laughs.

After a minute or so, she wiped away the tears that had leaked and retook Ellis's arm so they could return home. If she'd been asked that morning, she wouldn't have ever guessed that her afternoon would become a lasting memory—one that surpassed even her favorite ones of Margate and her grandmother.

And yet, despite her euphoria of the day, a shadowy place in her heart held firmly to all her doubts. She now knew without question that she loved Ellis, but he had yet to say anything about his own feelings. She thought that he cared, to some degree. But did he love her as well? Would anyone ever say that he was besotted with her?

She'd thought that regaining her parents' praise

and regard was difficult enough. If her parents, who undeniably loved her, could not find anything to praise about Clara, how could she possibly become the woman everyone knew Ellis loved?

When they returned home, Gregory and Lizzy waved from where they were snuggled up against their mother on the sofa, where she was reading to them from *Alice in Wonderland* again.

"Where's Harold?" Ellis asked. The small boy was conspicuous in his absence.

"He fell asleep on the way home," Eliza explained. "Mother went out to visit some friends, and Ronald is in your study answering some business inquiries. A message was dropped off for you as well. Ronald took it, so you'll need to ask him about it."

Ellis nodded, and once again, he became the practical doctor rather than the silly man who teased Clara and kissed her senseless in the dark.

Clara sighed and pushed aside her disappointment. As much as she enjoyed that aspect of him, she did appreciate his reliability. It simply meant that their unexpected free afternoon together truly was at an end.

No matter. She had made a promise to some children, and she was looking forward to fulfilling it.

They hadn't seen some of her more elaborate molds, like the tower of fruit or the pair of doves, since she kept those in the trunk in her room. They'd been delighted with her fish mold when she made the riplon and curry iced soufflé the other night.

"What kind of ice shall I make today?" she asked, clapping her hands together. "Strawberry? Ginger? Pear?"

"Do you have chocolate?" Lizzy was practically bouncing on her knees with hope and excitement.

"Do I have chocolate?" Clara playfully scoffed. "Why would I have something as delectable as chocolate? I only make horrible, nasty treats."

"May we have some, Aunt Clara?" Gregory joined in with the pleading. He'd pulled his feet underneath him and was squirming about.

"A horrible, nasty treat? I suppose... but only if you have a strong distaste for a strawberry mousse ice drizzled with chocolate syrup. And you must wait a horrendously long time for it to freeze, or else it'll come out a goopy mess."

Eliza grabbed both of her children by the hands and pulled them back into their seats on either side of her. "You must stop this jumping though. You'll ruin the upholstery on Aunt Clara's furniture, and then she won't be able to make you ices since she'll be out shopping for a new sofa."

Clara laughed and waved a dismissive hand. "I'll

leave you to handle their energy," she told Eliza over her shoulder as she walked out of the parlor.

In the kitchen doorway, she paused. She could hear paper crinkling and something that sounded suspiciously like a pencil. But Ellis's study was too far away for her to hear something as quiet as that. She stepped into the kitchen, listening intently.

A moment later, there was a long *riiiiippp* that came from the far side of the kitchen table and chairs.

Clara walked over and crouched to look under the edge of the table.

Harold looked up at her and grinned excitedly from the middle of a nest of torn pages from a book. "I made you a picture," he said, holding out a mangled sheet.

His fingers were covered in black ink, and he had a large splotch on his cheek.

"Oh, thank you," Clara said, blinking in mild shock.

Without thinking, she took the paper from him. "Does your father know you are in here? Your mother is reading *Alice* to the others. Do you want to join them?"

Harold crawled out and leaned against Clara. "I want to help you make the ices."

He was solidly built, so his weight threw her off-balance. She threw out her free hand to catch herself before she completely collapsed onto the floor and held Harold with the other, accidentally crumpling his picture.

"You want to help?" Clara asked. "I suppose so, but you should ask your mother first. And then we should clean up these papers. Can you tell me where you got them?"

She hoped that it was one of the children's books Ellis had instead of something from his study. Those were his medical texts that he kept on hand to reference.

"I got it from there," Harold said, pointing behind Clara.

"From there?" Clara twisted to see what he was pointing at.

Her heart sank, and she fell onto her rump.

It was her trunk that she hadn't bothered taking upstairs since she used it so often. She did have a few notebooks in it, but only one book that she referred to often enough to keep down in the kitchen.

She looked back at Harold, who was looking innocently back at her.

Clara swallowed, then licked her suddenly dry lips. "Let's look at the picture you drew me," she said.

Harold climbed into her lap and cheerfully began explaining his scribbles.

Clara only saw the remains of her treasured notes and recipes from Mrs. Marshall's *Book of Ices* hidden beneath those black marks. The hours—*years*—of effort she'd poured into her future success were in those pages so easily mangled by a curious boy's small hands.

The recipes would be easy enough to replace, even if she hadn't memorized many of them by now. But the memories, the dreams...

If she were unable to win Ellis's regard, that little book was all she had to remind her that she was capable. That she had another dream that was worthy of her attention.

Numb, she nodded and made some sort of encouraging sounds, but she couldn't begin to tell anyone what Harold was saying.

Finally, he stood up and helped her gather the pages before he wandered off. Presumably to find Eliza and ask her about helping Clara with the ices, but Clara couldn't bring herself to follow him.

"Clara, are you in here?"

She heard Ellis's footsteps as he approached the kitchen. Then, "Whatever are you sitting on the floor fo—? Oh."

She didn't look at him. She couldn't pull her eyes away from the carnage that once was her most treasured possession. She felt lost without it. She'd forgotten to protect her book, just like she was beginning to lose sight of her dream of an ices shop. How could Clara make anyone proud if she couldn't *do* anything worthy of their regard?

Ellis knelt next to her and pulled her into an embrace. "Clara, I am so sorry. I thought I heard a noise in here, and I should have checked."

She shook her head. "No, I should have put it somewhere safe. That was my responsibility, and I let myself forget."

Tears were forming, but Harold was coming back. She sniffled, then rubbed at her eyes. She wouldn't let this stop her. She would still find a way to enjoy making those children their ices, even if she had to fake being cheerful.

How had such a wonderful afternoon turned so quickly into something so horrible?

CHAPTER 14

When she recovered from her initial shock with the aid of a good cry, a night of sleep, and Ellis's murmured words of support, Clara began piecing together the torn pages of her cookbook. The Mathersons were extremely chagrined when they learned of Harold's post-nap activities and repeatedly apologized despite Clara's reassurances that she did not hold it against them or Harold. He was a curious little boy who still did not understand the implications of his actions. After a day or two of the Mathersons' apologies and regretful winces when they saw her working on her cookbook, Clara resolved to only continue in the privacy of her and Ellis's bedroom in the morning before their houseguests were up and in the evenings after they went to bed so the Mathersons wouldn't constantly be reminded.

When Ellis was home, he assisted her by transcribing her still-readable notes into a notebook that they ensured was placed on a higher shelf in their bedroom closet when they weren't around.

She truly didn't need most of the notes she'd made

at this point. With how frequently she practiced, she could make a number of those ices in her sleep. The ones she did need an actual recipe for were those she made so rarely that she doubted that she'd feel the loss. The repairs were more to remind herself of why she came to Margate in the first place—to make a name for herself that would make her family proud to speak of her.

The shop opened next week, and Clara was determined to do it right, regardless of what happened in her personal life.

Otherwise, she spent the mornings spending time with the Mathersons and Mrs. Archibald or visiting some of her new acquaintances in town, like the very helpful suppliers Mrs. Archibald introduced her to. The afternoons were devoted to preparing her shop for opening, including practicing making some of the simpler ices as rapidly as possible. Mrs. Marshall's Patent Freezer made the actual freezing of the ices happen in a matter of minutes, but the molded ices still needed an hour or two in the caves to solidify into their final shapes. Without actual customers, Clara was making her best educated guess on which ices would be most popular.

Inside the shop proper, the carpenters had installed new counters and shelves in the front area to her specifications and set up a kitchen in the back room. She'd even invested in having those new electric lights installed. Unfortunately, that particular endeavor took longer than she'd anticipated, so setting up for serving her future customers was running behind schedule.

Mrs. Archibald accompanied her on a couple of occasions to supervise the workmen and gave her some advice on suppliers and advertising, which Clara greatly appreciated. Marshall's School of Cookery did not cover much in the way of actually running a business.

On this particular afternoon, she was impatiently awaiting the delivery of more molds and food colorings from Mrs. Marshall's and the tablecloths from a local woman that Mrs. Stephens had recommended when Ellis asked for Clara. Workmen were currently maneuvering her largest iceboxes into their places in the kitchen area. They'd padded the edges with rough cotton coverings, but Clara still winced when they clipped the doorframe. Hopefully they hadn't scraped any of the fresh paint.

Someone knocked on the front door.

"Finally," she breathed out as she turned. Waiting on other people before she could do any of her own work was aggravating.

Her irritation vanished as soon as she saw Ellis standing in the doorway with his doctoring case. "May I join you?"

"Of course." She happily went to him and gave

him a quick kiss on his cheek while he set down his case. "This is your first time seeing it with the new paint and papering, yes?"

Ellis wasn't able to stop by the shop often, so seeing him lightened Clara's heart. She pulled him farther in, anxious to show him the improvements. Despite her pride in the changes, she needed his reassurances that she wouldn't fail—that her shop would be a success.

As her shop's opening approached, Clara was acutely aware of the distinct possibility of a larger scandal than the one she initially feared. Her parents sent a letter the other day confirming their arrival for the opening celebrations, which she kept hidden in her bag. They still did not know about Ellis, and Clara dreaded telling them all her lies. She wished she knew what would bring them the greater disappointment—the fact that she'd been so rash in moving into her new home without all the pertinent facts, or the fact that she lied to everyone around her to hide her initial mistake. She hoped that after meeting Ellis, their disappointment would be soothed.

Her husband was far better than she deserved.

Feeling sick at heart, Clara pressed closer to Ellis's side. As undeserving as she was, she still craved his strength and dependability. Without her parents' approval, she would be crushed. If she lost Ellis's support, she would shatter.

Ellis was looking at her, so she buried her fears again. Thinking of them only paralyzed her, and she had to be strong. Capable.

Praiseworthy.

"Once those iceboxes are in place, then I can have the larger ice deliveries begin," she told him, pointing in the direction of the kitchen area. Then she pointed at the counter where she intended to do demonstrations on opening day.

"I'm planning on setting up some displays of the more intricate ices there to illustrate what I am making, but I'm worried that they will take up too much room, and I won't have the space I need to work," she confessed.

Ellis nodded and pursed his lips. She loved the crinkle his brow got when he thought like that. It meant that he was seriously considering her words and was trying to come up with a solution for her.

"What if you were to get an artist or a photographer to come in? Then you could have both the room you need to work and a more permanent display for customers who would like to place custom orders?"

Clara liked where he was going. "Oh yes. Maybe that gentleman who took our photo in Ramsgate? He was charming and competent. Whatever happened to that, anyway?"

She remembered looking at the photo after the

photographer processed and gave it to them on their wedding day, but then Ellis had put it somewhere, and she'd gotten so busy that she'd forgotten about it.

Ellis frowned. "I thought you had it."

"No," Clara shrugged. "You had it on the train home. No matter. I'm sure it'll turn up. Do you think we'll be able to get any photographer or even an illustrator soon enough though? What of the cost?"

"Is your heart set on the Ramsgate photographer? Or at this point, would you prefer someone who can get the job done in time?"

Before Clara could answer, one of the workmen poked his head out of the kitchen area.

"Ma'am? The kitchen's too snug to get all your boxes to fit properly. Would you come look and tell us what you'd like done?"

Clara sighed in frustration. "I'll be there momentarily," she told him. After he disappeared, she held up her hands in a small gesture of frustrated helplessness.

"It's one thing after another," she ranted to Ellis. "I have a delivery that was supposed to arrive by this morning, but it's still not here. Then the display, and now this. If problems keep cropping up, I won't have any time to make enough ices before the shop opens."

Ellis took her by the arms near her shoulders and turned her to face him. Squeezing gently, he said, "Problems are normal. You're intelligent and hard-working. None of these will stop you from showing Margate the type of woman you are. Take care of that, then I have something for you."

Clara nodded resolutely and marched into the kitchen. Fortunately, the solution was figuratively easy. They simply had to move a counter opposite the iceboxes long enough for the workmen to slide the boxes into place. The workman who had fetched her reassured her that moving the counter was a matter of unscrewing a few bolts and that her kitchen would be returned to working order by quitting time that evening.

Annoyed at this hiccup, but still grateful that she *would* have her kitchen, Clara went back into the dining area. She was curious about what Ellis had for her.

While she'd been in the back, her delivery had finally arrived. Ellis was directing the man to put the boxes on her display counter and had purloined a couple of boys off the street to assist with the delivery.

"I wasn't sure where you wanted these," he told her with an apologetic smile when he saw her.

"There is perfect," Clara said fervently. "They have to dismantle a counter in the back, so I'd prefer not having more items in their way for the time being."

She signed off the delivery and began sorting through the boxes while Ellis paid off the boys once they brought in the last items. When quiet returned to the dining area, Clara paused her sorting and waited for Ellis.

He retrieved his case and pulled out a book wrapped in packaging paper. "I just picked this up at the train station after seeing off the family. Normally, I would have given this to you at home, but I couldn't help myself."

Confused, Clara took the book and unwrapped it.

"*Mrs. A.B. Marshall's Book of Cookery*," she read. "But this is—"

"Fresh from the press. Mother wrote a friend to get you a replacement for the one you lost, and they found this instead."

Clara clutched the book to her chest, speechless.

"I initially thought I'd wait until after your opening, but then I thought that it might have different recipes you could use for your shop..."

Clara stopped his rambling explanation with a hug. "Thank you, Ellis. I cannot begin to tell you how much this means to me."

Ellis smiled, then said, "I have one more patient to see before we go to the Coveys. Shall I meet you at home before we go?"

Clara nodded. "I'll be here for another hour or two, but I'm planning on changing before dinner."

Noises from the kitchen area reminded her that they weren't alone, so she settled for another quick kiss before Ellis left. Alone once again, she thumbed through the pages of her new book with excitement before setting it aside and resuming her task.

She wouldn't have thought that a new cookbook could bring her so much happiness. But this one was a sign of hope. A sign of Ellis's care and support for her. Regardless of what happened next week with her shop and her parents, her marriage of convenience might actually become a real love match.

CHAPTER 15

"Now, I'm not nearly so talented in the kitchen as our Clara," Mrs. Covey said as she led Clara, Ellis, and his mother into the Coveys' parlor that evening. "But I do like to flatter myself that I can hold my own."

"I'm sure it will be lovely," Mrs. Archibald said. She'd decided to stay until Clara's shop opened, and the Coveys had insisted on her joining their small dinner party.

"I promise I shan't think poorly of a single thing. How could I when you've been so generous and welcoming?" Clara said fervently. She'd been looking forward to this evening and seeing the Coveys and Mrs. Stephens again.

Ellis simply nodded. He'd retreated back into his unreadable form, which Clara now recognized as a sort of shield he donned around patients and their families. If they couldn't glean anything other than polite professionalism from him, they couldn't claim a further intimacy than he desired, nor could they make assumptions about his prognoses beyond what he told them. Clara was getting better at understanding her husband, but she still had a long way to go. One day in the future, would she be able to read his expressions regardless of his mask? How she hoped she would.

Mrs. Stephens was sitting in a wheeled bath chair with a wool blanket over her legs, chatting with another older couple. Mr. Covey sat off to the side by himself, watching.

"Mrs. and Mrs. Archibald," Mrs. Covey said, nodding at both Clara and her mother-in-law with amusement, "I don't believe either of you have met Mrs. and Colonel MacKenzie. Mr. Archibald, of course, is already quite familiar with them."

After they exchanged "How-do-you-dos," Mrs. Covey led them all into the dining room. The only noise was the quiet shuffling of chairs as they found their seats. Ellis and Mr. Covey helped Mrs. Stephens out of her bath chair, then while Ellis helped her get situated, Mr. Covey whisked the chair to another room where it would be out of the way.

"Where is Judith tonight?" Ellis asked Mrs. Stephens after he sat to her left. His mother sat to his other side, to Mr. Covey's right. Clara was opposite Mrs. Stephens, next to Mrs. Covey at the end of the table.

Mrs. Stephens leaned toward him, but her faux whisper was clearly audible. "I gave her the night off. Her beau's regiment is getting re-stationed in the morning. Such a shame. It's hard to be separated from your love, which I am sure you understand quite well." She patted him on the forearm and gave Clara a saucy wink.

Straightening, she told Clara, "I am sorry that we haven't had a chance to talk much since you came to town. But you undoubtedly wished to acclimate yourself to being a wife without a harridan such as myself inserting herself as soon as you arrived."

"Mother!"

"Mrs. Stephens, you are no such—"

Mrs. Covey and Clara responded at the same time.

Mrs. Stephens chuckled and reached across the corner of the table to grasp her daughter's hand. "Oh, I do love to rile you up, Rebecca. Positively wicked of me, I know."

Mr. Covey returned at that moment, so the conversation was momentarily paused while he said grace and dinner was started.

"Now, my dear," Mrs. Stephens jumped back into the topic. "Do tell me all that has been going on. Your mother kept me apprised for a time, but I haven't heard much in the last two to three years or so."

"Mr. Archibald," the colonel said loudly, disrupting Clara's thoughts. "I know you're an avid sportsman. What do you say to starting a footballers' league in Margate?"

Clara watched him from the corner of her eye. She had no idea what the man was on about. Ellis, an avid sportsman? He'd never so much as breathed a word about anything sporting-related.

Ellis paused, his soup spoon suspended midair. "Are you referring to rugby football? Or to association football—how do they refer to it at Oxford now—assoccer?"

Clara blinked. Apparently Ellis did know something about sporting.

The colonel grunted. "Rugger football. My nephew watched Seddon at work during the championships last year. Says it's the sort of rough and tumble sport needed for a hot-blooded man. This year's team is on tour in the penal colonies."

"Ah." Ellis nodded and resumed eating before answering further. "I believe that it would be a healthy form of exercise for many younger men, but I have no interest in getting tossed about. There are plenty of other calisthenics that provide the necessary benefits without the potential for brain injuries. I am sure my wife would prefer mine to stay as intact as possible."

"Bah," the colonel grumbled. "Didn't take you for a namby-pamby. Give me the man who would sleep in the mud, then charge the enemy as soon as word was given."

While he was speaking, Mrs. Covey leaned over to Clara and in an uncharacteristically low and sober tone, she said, "The poor colonel's mind is slowly going. More and more often, he'll believe himself just returned from the Crimean Peninsula and that he's a much younger man. Do not draw attention to anything he might say—the colonel is a proud man and is horribly embarrassed when his senses return. Our home is quickly becoming one of the only places the MacKenzies feel comfortable coming to."

Clara nodded, feeling both pity and sadness for the MacKenzies. It must be so difficult for them both. She looked across at Ellis, who responded to the colonel's comments as if he also had served in the Crimea. She was once again struck by gratitude and pride in her patient, caring husband.

For a time, they followed the colonel's lead and talked about sporting events, though Clara knew nothing about them. Clearly, sports were a familiar topic in the Covey and MacKenzie households. At first, Clara was intrigued and listened intently, but as the conversation continued and even Mrs. Archibald knew enough to chime in on occasion, Clara felt more like a forgotten observer.

Eventually, the topic drifted back into familiar realms, and Clara heaved a silent sigh of relief. She didn't have to be a wallflower any longer.

"My Agatha will have her lying-in in late summer, so I expect that I'll leave soon after Mr. Covey returns from Wales. This will be her seventh," Mrs. Covey said.

"Seven," Clara exclaimed. Mrs. Covey's daughter couldn't be much more than a year or two older than Clara. She couldn't imagine having that many children by this point, even if she had married far younger.

Mrs. Stephens must have guessed Clara's thoughts. "She's had two sets of twins. Apparently, they are common in his family," she explained.

"I imagine soon you'll be in a similar situation, Mrs. Archibald," Mrs. MacKenzie commented to Clara. "Least if you aren't already."

"Many registrar brides are, before the wedding," the colonel said matter-of-factly. "They skip the ceremony and go straight for the legalities to keep it quiet-like."

Mrs. MacKenzie turned scarlet. "I didn't mean to imply that was the case with you," she stammered quickly. "It's quite obvious looking at you that you aren't far enough along... I mean, I am sure both you and Mr. Archibald have... oh dear..." She trailed off.

"I know what you meant," Clara said, keeping her tone even. "And I am not offended. The colonel was simply stating a fact."

Yet another lie, but this was one she didn't feel guilty about telling. In truth, this was exactly the sort of gossip Clara had been steeling herself for ever since she agreed to marry Ellis. She hadn't anticipated it taking so long to come up though.

Mrs. Stephens cleared her throat. "Clara, have you heard when your family is arriving for your shop's opening? If they have the time, perhaps we could host another little get-together. The last time I saw the Wards, Michael was about this tall," she said, holding her hand up to indicate Michael's height to the rest of the dinner group.

Clara dabbed at her lips, trying not to squirm. What a fine pit she'd dug for herself. She couldn't tell Ellis about her parents' letter since he'd wonder at the lack of comment about their marriage. But she was growing tired of all the lies she had to tell to protect her reputation. Were any of them worth it?

"I'm sure they'll arrive a day or two before," she said. It wasn't exactly a lie. They had told her which trains they were most likely to take depending on when her father was able to finish his work as a banker.

Ellis was looking at her with his thinking face. Did he suspect anything?

"It's odd they haven't written or sent a telegram," he said, watching her eyes.

Clara fought to appear unconcerned. She was doomed. She really should confess to him, but she couldn't say anything now. Not with everyone else around. Between Mrs. Covey and her love of talking and the colonel's unpredictable state, word would surely spread.

"Perhaps their letter went astray?" she suggested,

then took a bite to avoid saying more.

Mrs. Covey and Mrs. Stephens exchanged looks, then Mrs. Stephens looked at Clara. "If you've had no word from your mother, you really must send her a telegram to confirm. She wouldn't want you to be unaware of her plans. In situations such as this, it isn't fair for either party to not know what's going on."

Clara forced herself to swallow. "Perhaps I shall," she said. Mrs. Stephens's words couldn't have made a bigger impact, even if she understood the full situation. There were so many people Clara was unintentionally injuring with her pride over her silly reputation. But looking at Ellis, with his far-too-perceptive expression, Clara knew.

While her lies might have saved her reputation, when the extent of them came out, they would cost her something far more valuable.

CHAPTER 16

T he next morning, Clara was still deeply unsettled. She needed a physical outlet for her internal agitation—something that allowed her body to release energy while her mind focused on other matters, so she left not long after waking up to make ices in her shop.

Mrs. Stephens's words repeated themselves over and over in Clara's mind while she turned the crank on an ice freezer in the otherwise silent shop.

It isn't fair for either party to not know what's going on.

She really wasn't being fair to either Ellis or her parents. They deserved to know about him, and he did not deserve to be kept hidden away. If Clara met him in more agreeable circumstances, she would have practically dragged her parents to meet him at the soonest opportunity possible.

She had to do right by all of them.

Her parents, no matter their disappointment, would still be there for her. She'd simply have to give them time.

As for Ellis... well, she had no idea how he would respond.

They'd rarely spoken of matters that actually meant something to each other. For all that they lived under the same roof and shared the same bed, they'd rarely actually shared their innermost thoughts and desires with each other. Ellis rarely volunteered his, and given the nature of their marriage, Clara felt as if she had already required too much from him. Asking for a more emotional or deeper commitment was not the easy marriage of convenience Ellis had agreed to. He was willing to be friends. He'd said as much the day they married. But he wanted a marriage where they would both go about their own business without having to worry about the other's needs.

Then she had to be silly enough to fall in love with the man. Love inherently requires more than proximity to live, much less thrive.

She pushed hard at the crank, forcing her frustration and confusion into the effort. Then she paused. Ices did not require this level of effort to crank. She sighed and checked on the contents.

Useless.

This was far too thick to use in a molded ice like she intended. She placed her hands on her hips and stared at the offending iced cream.

Her shop was supposed to be the answer to her problems, a chance for her to be worthy of praise and glory. Instead, she'd only created more problems and felt farther than ever from being someone praiseworthy.

She frowned and pulled out a spoon. No sense in letting this go to waste. A good ice might help her feel better.

She sat on a stool next to the counter and pulled the well full of blueberry ice toward her and began eating. She stared out at the now-completed interior of her shop. In this lighting, the window was highly reflective, and it appeared as if she were sitting at a table with her ice.

She faintly smiled at the sight. She'd tried so hard to imagine herself in this position the day she arrived. She'd even included an imaginary husband.

Now, she was married and hopelessly, irrevocably in love with someone who had married her to fix her own mistake. And her parents were unaware of the whole situation. She should have swallowed her pride and left Margate, or even dealt with the gossip and scandal of unknowingly staying a single night under the same roof with a bachelor. Now, even if Margate never knew about her lies, her own knowledge tainted her efforts.

She groaned and lay her forehead on the counter.

The bell above the door tinkled, and Clara sat up, embarrassed to be caught in this state.

"Are... you feeling well?" Ellis asked, looking as

confused as could be expected in this situation.

She half-heartedly shrugged. "Well enough. My thoughts are just in a jumble."

Ellis nodded in sympathy. "I'm sure. With your shop opening in just a few days, you must be feeling strained with all that you've been doing. But my mother was telling me last night that she believes you've set yourself up wonderfully and that opening will be a grand success."

Clara gave him a weak smile and poked her spoon at her hard ice. "Only if I can get myself back in order and actually make ices the way they're meant."

He followed her gaze to the ice. "Blueberry?"

His tone was amused, and it took Clara a moment to realize why—he was thinking of their banter over bad blueberries the day they got married. The fact that he even remembered such a trivial moment soothed Clara's turmoil enough for her to try a quip. "It *is* later in the season. You'll find no bad berries in my ices."

Ellis hmmed doubtfully. "How can you be sure if you aren't willing to test them yourself?"

Clara chuckled. "Who's to say that I haven't?"

He gave her a significant look, then leaned against her counter, looking far more relaxed than she'd seen him look in a while. "I saw how you snubbed those earlier berries. Wouldn't even give them the time of day."

"Unlike some," she drawled out, "I have a keenly

honed sense of taste and good sense when it comes to food."

"Ah, but is the ultimate prize not worth the effort?" He stuck a finger in her ice and scooped out a large glob.

"Excuse me, sir," she said with false indignation and gave his hand a light swat. "I'll thank you to keep your grimy hands out of my ices."

Ellis simply stuck his finger with the ice in his mouth and smirked at her. His eyes gleamed with humor and something else that Clara couldn't name. Whatever it was, it filled her with pleasure far more satisfying than her ices.

"Will you also thank me for some news I believe you'll be excited about?"

Curiosity piqued, Clara set down her spoon and sat up straighter. "And what is this news?"

Ellis shifted so he was directly facing her. "I was able to track down our Ramsgate photographer, and he's agreed to take photos of your offerings tomorrow afternoon—on condition that he also gets a free dessert." This last bit Ellis said with a wink.

Clara gaped at him. He'd done that for her? How? *When* did he even have the time to? They'd only thought of the idea yesterday afternoon. Her gratitude shifted into guilt. He had patients to see yesterday, but he'd somehow managed to squeeze in time to track down their unnamed photographer and get a response, while she neglected to write her own parents.

Ellis watched her. His own excitement faded from his eyes into wariness. "Of course, we don't want you getting overwhelmed with all that you have left to do by adding more," he offered, concern in his voice.

"Oh, it's not that," Clara said hastily. "I am simply... amazed and... and... the *effort*, Ellis. You didn't need to go through that for me."

"It was no bother. I'm happy to help. I want to see your shop succeed." Ellis took her hand. "It's the reason you came to Margate, and I've seen how hard you've been working. If my finding a photographer could lessen your worries, I want to do it."

His sincerity nearly broke Clara.

"I don't—" She was on the verge of confessing—of telling him that she did not deserve his kindness or him—when the bell above the door jingled.

Both Ellis and Clara turned to look at the intruder.

"I've a telegram for a Clara Ward?" The messenger boy held up the envelope as if he were proving his legitimacy.

"Yes, that's me," Clara said, standing. Dread weighed on her. Very few people who knew her as Clara Ward also knew the shop's address. She could count them on one hand. Whatever was in the message did not bode well.

Ellis was faster and took the telegram. "Thank you, young man," he said, dismissing him. He raised an eyebrow as he handed the envelope to Clara.

She studiously avoided looking him in the face while she opened it.

On train to Margate. Stay safe. AW

Clara closed her eyes. She was too late. Her parents were already on their way, and given her father's warning to stay safe, they somehow knew.

"Clara?"

She opened her eyes. Ellis was watching her again. His brow was furrowed, and he looked as if he might reach out to catch her. She had little doubt that she looked pale.

"My parents are on their way," she said faintly. Why had she let the situation get this far? Where was her courage when she most needed it?

"Would you like me to interfere? You need not see them," Ellis said with firmness.

"What?" Clara blinked, forcing herself out of her own mind.

"As your husband, I can restrict your parents' access to you. You could stay in the house with my mother, and I can meet them either at the station or the door and send them back home."

She'd never seen Ellis this intense before. It was as if he were stifling anger. And why would he want to prevent her from seeing her parents?

"That won't be necessary," she said.

"I don't care for the thought of them staying in our home. Not so unexpectedly and right before your shop opens. But I will do my best to shield you from them," he said.

"Why would I need shielding from my own parents?" Clara blurted. She was so confused. Was Ellis really going to prevent her from seeing her family, especially when his own had no problems dropping in unannounced?

Ellis gave her a strange look. "You always seem so... uncomfortable whenever they're brought up. And they never sent any sort of response about our wedding. What sort of parent can induce such feelings in their daughter?"

Clara groaned and covered her face with her hands. This was spiraling far beyond what she'd imagined the consequences to be. "You misunderstand. My parents are wonderful, loving, and supportive people. They never responded to our wedding because I never wrote them about it."

"You never wrote them?"

Clara morosely shook her head.

"You mean that you never told them anything about how we were married? Simply that we were?" He sounded as baffled as he looked.

He didn't understand.

Ellis thought so well of her that he couldn't comprehend her deception. The shame was nearly overpowering. She forced herself to say the words that would forever dispel whatever good feelings he had. "No, Ellis. My parents still believe that I am single. They do not know of your existence."

Then she waited for his reaction, watched him for the disappointment that surely he must be feeling.

Instead, he blinked, a deep crease between his brows. "You really did not write them? At all? Why? If they are so supportive, then why not tell them? None of this makes sense, Clara."

"How could I? What was I supposed to tell them? That due to my stupidity, I am now in a disaster of a marriage—"

Even as Ellis reared back, hurt flashing across his face before that detestable, impassive doctor facade replaced it, Clara regretted her thoughtless words.

"Ellis, I'm sorry. That's not what I meant..." She reached out for him, but he withdrew his arm from her touch.

"But it is the first descriptor you thought of," he said evenly. Dispassionately. He might as well have been diagnosing her with a simple cold.

"It's not what I meant," she said again, feeling helpless. How could she begin to make him understand how important her reputation had been to her? How his regard now meant more to her than anything in the world, including her shop and any praise she might have garnered?

"So you've said." Ellis stooped to retrieve his case, then headed toward the door. "I will not intrude anymore."

Clara hurried around the counter, stumbling over her skirt and stools. "Please wait," she called after him.

He simply nodded toward her ices. "You are already behind. You've worked this hard already. Don't let me prevent you from finishing."

Then he was gone.

Clara reached the door far too late. She stepped out onto the street and looked for him in the crowds that passed by, unaware of her pain and regret. She didn't know which direction he would have gone.

"Ellis," she called again, straining her eyes for any sign of a reaction from the men walking away from her shop.

She earned herself curious or disapproving looks, but nothing from the one person she yearned for.

"Ellis," she whispered hopelessly. She hugged herself and kept searching. When even she could not make up reasons for why he might still be within sight or sound, she slumped and returned to the inside of her shop.

The well full of melty, sludgy blueberry ice sat on the counter, mocking her.

All the ices in the world couldn't make this right.

And her parents would be arriving soon.

CHAPTER 17

F ar too soon, Clara was fidgeting with her gloves on the train platform. The train whistle blew, and conductors walked up and down the platform, reminding people to step back as the train pulled in with squealing brakes and giant puffs of thick black smoke.

Clara's thoughts were nearly as thick and dark. After Ellis left, she'd cleaned up her shop, then returned home, hoping to find him there. When she didn't see him, she hurried to his office and was greeted by a "Closed" sign. Not knowing what else she could do, she'd slunk home in shame and mindlessly made ices. She'd perked up at every little creak from the house or the sound of voices out on the street. Each time, she was met with disappointment.

Even Mrs. Archibald hadn't seen Ellis by the time Clara had to leave. Clara forced back her tears and the tightness in her throat. Years ago, before she'd traded dreams of marital bliss for recipes and ingredients, she'd always imagined what it might be like to introduce a beau to her parents.

Now, she only had an upset and absent husband.

It appeared she would face the consequences of her choices on her own. As was only right and fair, no matter how much she wished Ellis were by her side.

Doors all along the cars opened, and passengers climbed down the steps while those waiting to greet them surged forward. Clara placed a hand over her middle and took deep breaths, willing her emotions to settle.

She felt a light touch on her elbow and turned.

"Ellis!"

She nearly threw herself at him, but at the last moment, she checked herself as Ellis took a half step back.

"As your husband, I should be here to greet your parents," he said stiffly, looking past her toward the wave of passengers hugging their loved ones or collecting their luggage.

"What I said earlier, Ellis..." Clara trailed off. She wanted to apologize, but any sign of openness was completely gone from Ellis. He'd been easier to approach when he was nothing more than a nameless intruder in her home. She might as well be speaking to one of the cliffs on the beach for all that he appeared to be listening.

"Clara!"

Both of them turned toward the cry.

Clara's mother uncharacteristically shoved her

way through the crowd. Her father, weighed down by a couple of carpetbags, was not far behind.

Seeing them, the urge to cry from both relief and guilt was almost too much for her. When her mother threw her arms around Clara with a quiet "You're safe," her self-control broke. Tears leaked out of her eyes faster than preferred, but she'd have to let go of her mother to dig out her handkerchief, and she simply could not bring herself to do that.

Something soft nudged her hand. Ellis still wasn't looking at her, but he held out his own handkerchief while he waited for her to accept it.

"Thank you, Ellis," she whispered and accepted his offering, still clinging to her mother.

Her father arrived with an intense, distrustful look at Ellis.

Clara disentangled herself from her mother and dabbed at her eyes. "I'm so happy to see you both," she said. "Also, I owe you an apology, but before we get into that, we should do introductions. This is Ellis Archibald, my husband."

"Arthur Ward." Clara's father shook Ellis's hand, but based on the subtle tightening around both of the men's eyes, Clara knew the gesture was far from friendly.

"And my mother, Mercy Ward," she interjected before her father could do anything else.

Her mother's greeting was more pleasant but still

lacked the warmth that she typically displayed.

How was it possible for reality to outdo even Clara's worst imaginings? She'd assumed her parents would be upset, but she never thought they would be angry with her husband. Of course, she'd also thought she was braver and more honest than what she'd proven herself to be, and look how she'd disproved herself.

"Shall we go to the house?" Clara asked with false cheeriness. She glanced toward Ellis, hoping that he would extend his arm to escort her as he had so many times in the last few weeks. Her fear that he wouldn't was spot-on. Instead of looking at her, he was flagging down a porter.

Clara's parents took advantage of Ellis's distraction and looped their arms around hers. She craned her head over her shoulder, watching her husband.

"Have Mr. and Mrs. Ward's belongings taken to number 8, Scarborough Lane," he instructed the porter. His gaze flicked toward Clara, and she glimpsed the real Ellis—the one who cared for her and was hurting. Then, he waved her and her parents off.

"I'll see to the baggage and rejoin you shortly," he said briskly.

Her mother nodded in acknowledgement while her father started off, subtly tugging on Clara's arm.

Tension was radiating from all three of them,

but Clara was unwilling to discuss anything of real importance out on the street where anyone might overhear them. Instead, she kept up a running monologue about the people she'd met and how the set-up for her shop's opening was going.

She kept glancing behind them for Ellis, but it took him a while to make a reappearance. When he did, he strolled along with his hands in his trouser pockets. Clara's mother also noticed Ellis's half-hearted attempt to catch them and exchanged a concerned look with her husband.

Clara would happily—gratefully, even—take being physically ill over this torment.

By the time all four of them reached Clara's home, she'd talked herself hoarse, and she was ready to collapse into bed. A bed that, unfortunately, she shared with a man she'd deeply offended, who wouldn't even look her in the eyes.

Mrs. Archibald met them in the front hallway with a cheerful smile while the smell of dinner wafted out of the kitchen. Her expression faltered as she took in Clara's distress and Ellis's aloofness, but she quickly masked her concern with a welcome.

"You must be Mr. and Mrs. Ward. I'm Ellis's mother, but please, call me Eunice." She clasped both of their hands, and Clara stifled her sigh of relief as her mother's frostiness visibly melted under Mrs. Archibald's attention.

"I expect you'll want a few minutes to settle in and refresh before we eat," Mrs. Archibald said while she bustled them all into the parlor. "Clara, would you mind pouring the tea? I have some biscuits in the oven that I thought might go well with one of your ices later tonight."

The distraction was much needed. It gave Clara something to do with her hands and a reason to avoid looking at her parents. She'd just handed Ellis his tea, her fingers brushing against his as he took the cup, when she saw someone leaving the street and heading toward their front door.

"Oh dear." She really did sigh this time. "It's Drutherson again."

After their initial meeting, where Clara had to introduce herself without Ellis there, Mr. Drutherson stopped by at least twice a week on behalf of his employer.

Ellis went to meet the man at the door and came back within a minute. "Mr. Drutherson is actually worried—she took a serious tumble. Don't wait up for me." Then he was gone again.

Clara's parents stared at the empty doorway while Clara turned to watch him rush down the front steps with Mr. Drutherson. He'd told her not to wait up for him. Did that mean he wasn't too upset and simply needed time? Or was that a hint that he didn't want to see her, and he was considerate enough to continue their ruse of a loving marriage, at least for now?

The silence lengthened. Her father coughed, and her parents looked at her expectantly. She knew what they were waiting for, but she needed another moment to recollect herself.

Noises from the kitchen were a reminder that they weren't entirely alone. Clara didn't need Mrs. Archibald walking in on her apology. "I'll show you to your room," she said, standing.

She took them to what used to be her room. As it was the furthest from her and Ellis's room, Clara felt it the most prudent option, given her father's animosity to her husband. The fact that the room had a pretty view of the sea was an extra perk.

"Clara," her mother said as soon as they entered the room. "We need to know—"

"I know. I should have told you sooner," Clara blurted. "But I was too embarrassed and didn't want you to be ashamed of me."

"Ashamed? Clara." Her father sounded both surprised and exasperated. "Mrs. Stephens wrote us and mentioned that you were married. We had no idea what kind of man you'd found yourself trapped by or if you were even safe."

Mrs. Ward laid a calming hand on her husband's arm. "I'm sorry we ever gave the impression that you couldn't come to us for help, especially in a situation like this. We love you and want you to be happy."

Clara wrapped her arms around her middle. She felt all sorts of foolish. She was no better than one of the Matherson children with her behavior, and they at least had the legitimate excuse of their ages.

Mrs. Ward sat on the edge of the bed and patted the spot next to her. "Please, tell us what's going on."

"If you need a divorce, we will help you with that. There's no need to stay with that man another night," her father grumbled. "We can stay at one of the hotels tonight and be gone on the first train back home."

Clara gasped. Divorce?

"Arthur," her mother chided. "Let's hear Clara out before we leap to any extremes—although, Clara darling, if you do want to leave, just say the word."

Clara was already shaking her head. "No," she said vehemently. "I don't want to leave. Oh, this is all such a mess."

She placed her head in her hands, clenching her hair. If she had a pillow and solitude, she'd scream into it.

She took a deep breath, then let it out slowly. It was time for her to face her faults. She sat up and told her parents everything.

"And now, I don't know what to do. I love him, but he never agreed to this kind of arrangement. I've been horribly selfish and far too much of a coward. He doesn't deserve to be tied to me for the rest of his life, but the thought of... of actually leaving him... or putting him through that scandal when he was only trying to protect my reputation in the first place... I just can't." She collapsed backward onto the bed and stared up at the ceiling.

The position was highly undignified, but as far as she was concerned, she already had lost all dignity. Her father had been pacing around the room while she spoke, poking into various nooks and crannies. She supposed her need to move when working out difficult problems came from him. If only she had more of her mother's poise and ability to be level-headed.

Her mother lay on her side next to Clara and stroked her hair. "What if that's what Mr. Archibald wants?"

Clara shrugged, her despondency making her apathetic. "Then I suppose I must. He's done so much for me... I would do anything to make him happy."

Mr. Ward was frowning at an open book in his hands. "I don't believe that would make him happy," he said. He turned around as he pulled out something from the pages, then held it out to Clara and her mother.

Mrs. Ward took it while Clara sat up and peeked over her mother's shoulder.

"That—" Mr. Ward said emphatically, pointing at the paper, "is not the expression of a man who married for convenience."

Clara's mother held the photograph from

Ramsgate.

"Oh my," she said softly, holding it out so they both could see. "You look radiant."

Clara knew she'd seen the photo before, but she didn't think she'd actually *looked* at it. Her mother's description was accurate—her smile, captured mid-laugh, was the largest, freest expression of joy she'd ever seen. And Ellis...

Clara's fingers trembled while she took the photo from her mother. How had she not noticed before? If she didn't know what happened that day, she would describe his expression as besotted. Still... She couldn't ignore the adoration in his eyes. Not when the expression was frozen by paper and chemicals like this. She touched his face in the photo, tracing his features with her eyes.

Did he actually feel that way? Could he still feel that adoration for her, even after she'd used him so poorly?

Mrs. Ward touched the back of Clara's hand. "I think," she said slowly, looking at her own husband for confirmation, "that your marriage has been a lie, but not in the way you think it was."

"Tell me," Mr. Ward said. "How typical was Mr. Archibald's behavior, starting from when we met him?"

Clara furrowed her brow. She must have done a terrible job explaining Ellis's reaction to her omission.

"I've never seen him upset like this," she said.

Her father gave a sharp nod and slapped his thighs while he sat on the other side of Clara. "Right, then. That settles it. Your mother and I know nothing about your husband, but we do know human nature, and an indifferent man would not be fazed by your actions, much less hurt to this degree. So, if you want him to *stay* your husband, then you must be the one to fix this."

"But I don't know how," Clara exclaimed. "He won't listen to me. Not anymore."

Mr. Ward huffed in disbelief. "Rubbish."

"Men who do not care for their wife's opinion wouldn't tell her he might be out late." Her mother looked at her with loving sternness. "I'll wager that he wants to fix this as much as you do. Now, take your indomitable spirit that got you through that school of yours and into a position where you are a woman of business and figure this sticky situation out."

She stood and pulled Clara to her feet before giving her a hug and lightly pushing her toward the door. "We do need to refresh ourselves before dinner, and *you* need some time to think."

In the corridor, Clara clutched the photo to her chest, her mother's words sinking further into her with each heartbeat.

Her parents believed in her. They believed Ellis loved her.

She could salvage her marriage. Somehow.

CHAPTER 18

C lara checked her watch pin. It was nearly one in the morning, and Ellis still hadn't returned home. Based on the increased crashing of the waves, a storm was rolling in. Was he still seeing to that woman? Had he finished and something else prevented him from returning home? Or were they all wrong and Ellis didn't intend to return to Clara? She was likely to go mad from the uncertainty.

She checked on the pork pies she'd made after everyone else retired for the night. She'd thought Ellis might not want a full meal coming home so late, but she wouldn't let him go to bed hungry. Who knew the last time he ate something filling?

How she despised indefinite waiting.

She'd already cleaned the kitchen within a spot of its life, so she couldn't use that to wear out her emotions. But she wouldn't sleep until she knew that Ellis was safe. She was afraid that if he were any later, they both would be too tired or overwrought to talk.

Without a better occupation, Clara pulled out her ice equipment. She was behind on what she needed to have ready for her shop anyway, thanks to the events of the day.

The measuring, pouring, and mixing of ingredients did help the time pass ever so slightly faster, but she froze at every creak or groan of the house's floorboards, hoping Ellis had returned.

Finally, she heard the noise she'd been wordlessly praying for.

She quickly wiped her hands on her apron and pulled it off her head, throwing it on top of the cold stovetop as she rushed out of the kitchen.

"You're home," she said, feeling herself sag as her worries for him left.

"What are you doing up so late?" Ellis whispered, more of a dark shape against the night's shadows. The only light was coming from the kitchen, but Clara could have sung, seeing him reach for her.

"I needed to see you," she said. She grasped him with both of her hands and gently pulled him toward the kitchen. "Are you hungry?" she asked, already bustling over to get him a plate. "Your mother cooked dinner that I can warm up for you, or there are pork pies."

Ellis stood in the doorway, watching her with confused wariness.

Clara completely understood the sentiment. She wasn't sure how to act around him either, not when it was just the two of them, and she still didn't know how he would respond when she laid her heart out for him.

What even was normal in this kind of situation?

"Come eat," she urged him, setting her platter of pies on the table. "It's been hours since you left."

Ellis didn't protest. While he ate, Clara got a kettle going for him before returning to her abandoned ice.

It was almost comfortable.

Once Ellis wiped his fingers with a napkin and sat back with his tea, Clara knew she had to speak now, or this opportunity would be gone. He watched her expectantly, waiting for her next move.

She took a deep breath. It was time to be the bravest she'd ever been.

"I... was not very clear earlier," she said, setting aside the ice freezer she'd been turning. "When I called our marriage a disaster, I only meant myself. If we had married for lo—if we'd known each other and had a mutual affection, I couldn't ask for a better husband. I still don't understand why you chose to help me when you very easily could have tossed me out. Repeatedly, you've proved yourself far beyond what I ever expected from our agreement. And I became greedy. I wanted more than our arrangement and was afraid of what others, of what *you* might think or say if I spoke of what I truly wanted."

Ellis was still. Observing. Analyzing.

The table was between them, both a barrier and

a shield. As much as she wanted to hide her fear that
Ellis didn't want more with her, she had to be open.
She walked around the table until she stood in front
of him. Her knees shook beneath her, but as nervous
as she was, she continued.

"We had a business arrangement, Ellis. And
somehow, it turned into something more. I fell in
love with you and the thought of you regretting your
choice has haunted me, day and night. Even when
I'm happily making my ices, watching my dreams take
shape around me, I find myself anxious to come home
to you. But... I can't expect any more from you than
what you've already given me. I have been the biggest
nuisance already. If you wish to be free again, I can
pack my things and be gone in the morning. I will take
all the blame so your reputation remains whole, as you
deserve."

Ellis cocked his head to the side, considering her.

When he didn't respond, Clara's heart sank. He
wasn't immediately declining her offer. She nodded
her acceptance. "I understand. Marriage to someone
like me was never something you'd have considered if
I hadn't been so hasty—"

Ellis abruptly stood, holding his fingers over her
mouth, silencing her. After a moment, he lowered his
hand until it found hers. He kissed her fingertips, then
clasped her hand between both of his, holding it to his
chest. He stared at her with a mix of fear and passion

so intense that she couldn't look away even while she blushed.

"You're right. You're not the kind of woman I ever imagined of marrying, even if I were more romantically inclined. This started as a marriage of convenience. A solution to our mutual difficulties. And being married to you has been anything but convenient. Ah"—he shook his head when she opened her mouth to apologize—"I'm not finished. You have invaded my home, disrupted my plans, steamrolled every attempt at keeping our lives separate, and I won't have it any other way. Before you came in with your bold dreams and chaotic emotions, I had settled for a staid life. You've reminded me what it is to live, to dream, to hope. But most of all, you've taught me how to love with a deeper part of my soul than I ever knew existed. If you leave, I will resume the same activities as before. If you leave, I'll return to my colorless life with the knowledge of what it was like to live in the rainbows. I can't imagine a more agonizingly slow death—knowing you are somewhere out there while I remain with a meaningless life and a heart slowly bleeding out."

Clara gaped at him, her feet rooted to the ground while she tried to wrap her head around his words. "Are... are you sure you're not romantically inclined?" she finally squeaked out. "Because I don't know how else to describe that."

Ellis smirked and wrapped his arms around her, pulling her closer.

Clara laid her head on him, reveling in the moment. "I'm asleep, aren't I?" she murmured. "I will wake up and discover that I dozed off in one of my ices and feel all sorts of disappointment and embarrassment."

His chest rumbled beneath her cheek while he chuckled. "If so, I should like to be the one who discovers you. But we should be going to bed if you want to avoid dozing off later today."

Clara hmmed, unconvinced. "I think I need more proof this is real," she said.

"I'll see what I can do," Ellis said before covering her with kisses that Clara couldn't possibly have dreamed of.

The next few days sped past Clara in a haze of euphoria and frantic, last-minute preparations. Now, she stood inside her shop with Ellis, her parents, and Mrs. Archibald by her side while her shopgirls made small adjustments to her display of ices and the Ramsgate photographer set up his camera in the corner before they officially opened the doors to customers.

Clara was running through her mental checklist. She was convinced that she'd forgotten something crucial.

"Are you sure that we have enough pressed napkins?" she asked Mrs. Archibald. "The crowd outside is much bigger than I thought it would be."

"Don't worry about the napkins," her mother-in-law soothed her. "You focus on enjoying yourself and seeing all your hard work pay off. We will handle those minor details."

There was a tapping at the door, which rattled Clara's nerves even more. "They're getting impatient, aren't they?"

"I think you'll want to let these particular customers in early," her father said, smiling at the window.

Clara turned around to see her brother Michael leaning in the front window, waving at her with an excited grin.

"Ellis—?" she began to ask.

"I've got crowd control handled," he said, already weaving around tables and chairs for the door. He opened it just enough for her brother to squeeze through, followed by a young woman, holding on to his hand so they wouldn't get separated.

"Just a few moments more," Ellis told someone through the gap. "It will be well worth the wait."

"Clara," Michael exclaimed. "Look at you! A married woman and now a bona fide shopkeeper."

They embraced. "I didn't think you were going to

make it," Clara said.

Her brother gave a nonchalant hug. "I couldn't miss this."

The young lady he was with gave an apologetic smile. "I'm afraid his delay is entirely my fault."

Michael scrunched up his nose. "Now, Mols, you had no control over your test dates."

Ellis rejoined Clara, having successfully mollified the people at the front of the crowd. He placed a hand on the small of her back, leaving her with a tingle where his hand rested. "You have a few more minutes before the chaos will be unleashed," he warned her.

She looked at him gratefully and wrapped her hand around his arm. Having him and the rest of her family nearby was more of a relief than she thought.

"Michael, this is my husband, Ellis Archibald," she told her brother.

"Pleasure," Michael said, enthusiastically shaking hands with him. "This is Mollie Hunt, my fiancée."

"Fiancée," Clara exclaimed. "And you thought you were just going to surprise me with that sort of news?" she teased him.

"At least it was before the wedding," he retorted with a wink.

"You deserved that," Ellis mumbled in Clara's ear.

She shook her head at him, then turned to Miss Hunt. "There is still time to retreat. I'm afraid you are unprepared for the trouble my brother truly is."

Miss Hunt laughed. "Oh, I am well aware of his penchant for mischief. But I will give him credit; he's done you no disservice, and I have been very eager to meet you."

"Oh?" Clara asked, looking between her brother and Miss Hunt.

"Nothing terrible, I assure you," Miss Hunt said. "Merely that he might as well not have existed for all the attention he received compared to you."

Clara raised her eyebrows in surprise. "You really thought that?" she asked her brother.

"Of course," he said. "That's about ninety percent of my childhood memories. Everyone talking about how bold you were, how intelligent and kind. Nobody could say enough about how much they admired you. And every bit of it is true."

Clara laughed in amused disbelief. "And here I've been, thinking the same about you."

Noise from outside distracted her, and she looked toward the window. "I should get in place," she told them. "I have reserved the table over there for family. When Mrs. Stephens and Mrs. Covey arrive, please let me know," she said to Ellis.

"Of course," he said.

Clara straightened her crisp apron and stood next to the counter with her shopgirls. "Are you ready?" she asked them.

"Yes, ma'am," they answered, excitement lighting

their eyes.

Clara looked at Ellis, who had retaken his place by the front door. He gave her a nod, his pride showing even across the room.

She smiled back and gestured for him to let in the crowd. As the first of her customers swept in through the doors, Clara couldn't help but remember how she'd felt coming in town. Her happiness then was nothing compared to what she felt today. Pride and gratitude were bursting through her. Without her family's help and support, without Ellis by her side, none of this would have happened. Most of all, what filled Clara's heart the most was knowing that she, Clara Archibald, was loved.

A Note on Victorian Ices

Agnes B. Marshall was an incredible Victorian business woman. Like Clara, she benefitted from new laws and a supportive husband, and was able to run an extremely successful business. Or rather, businesses. On top of her school, she also ran her own product line for molds, flavors and colorings, and other equipment needed for making ices. It is also entirely possible that she created what we now refer to as the "ice cream cone." Agnes also published her own cooking, homemaking and gossip journal called *The Table.*

Ice(s) – We typically would think of these as "ice cream," but Victorian ices didn't necessarily use cream in all their ices. Some bases were "water and perfumed ices." Recipes for these are similar to how we would make a non-dairy smoothie. Many ices were sweet, but Victorians had a taste for more savory ices as well, including, yes, iced curry soufflés (which contain apple, curry, fish, and prawns).

Ice cave – Similar to today's freezers. These were boxes with ice and salt-insulated sides that would keep molded ices frozen up to a few days.

Icebox – A refrigerator that was frequently used to keep ice from melting too quickly.

Patent freezer – Similar to today's bucket ice

cream makers. This had an ingredient pan that sat in a bucket over a thin layer of salt and ice. A paddle inside the pan stirred the contents (via a hand crank on the lid). The thinner the contents, the faster the cream would freeze, so these freezers could get very wide. Reportedly, they were actually more efficient than today's home ice cream makers.

Acknowledgements

This book came at a time when I desperately needed something fun, lighthearted, and less daunting than the other projects I'd been working on. It's been an absolute delight writing this story and working with the other authors in the Victorians at the Beach series: Sienna Peake, Amy Newbold, Heloise C. Kensington, and Karen M. Edwards.

Madisyn at Mountain Peak Editorial took my extremely vague descriptions and worked some stunning design magic for this cover.

Many thanks to Meghan Hoesch for her copy edits.

After her work on my debut book, *Of Jasmine and Roses*, I am thrilled that Noah Wall has agreed to do the narration for this one as well.

A special thanks to Anthony Lee and his fabulous resource, https://www.margatelocalhistory.co.uk/. I've spent countless minutes (probably hours at this point—I've honestly lost track) pouring over the photos, maps, and articles absorbing everything I could to bring Margate to life. One of these days I'll be able to visit in person!

I'd still be wallowing in my personal "Pit of Despair" or doom-scrolling without my angelic friends' and family's encouragement. Thank you,

Rachel Hansen, Julia Allen, Rachel Stones, and the whole Warner and Bickham hordes for your support, especially my husband, Nathan, who repeatedly talked about my plot and writing blocks with me. A huge hug and even bigger thank you to the most patient of beta readers, Anneka Walker, Karen Thornell, and Jennifer Lanning. Sorry you had to wait forever and a day for the ending!

And as always, the biggest thanks goes to my Heavenly Father who never fails to answer my prayers, even if I forget to trust Him or can't quite follow his promptings.

About the Author

When she was little, Jill thought she would end up being a world-famous actress-baker-author while simultaneously being a stay-at-home mom. Since then, Jill has earned a BA in English and editing from Brigham Young University and worked as a web designer/web content developer. Now she's a stay-at-home mom who leaves the dramatics for the page, bakes on the smallest whim, and occasionally will actually write.

You can keep in touch with Jill by following her Instagram account (@jillewarner), subscribing to her newsletter on Substack https://jillewarner.substack.com/ (please note you only need to provide your email via the orange "Subscribe" button and do NOT need to create an account), or visiting her website http://www.jillewarner.com.

Also by Jill E. Warner

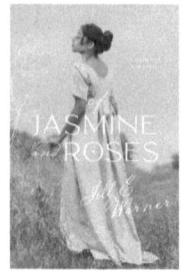

Orphaned as a child, Anna Beasley was raised alongside her titled cousin in the high Society of the ton. But part-Indian Anna knows better than anyone that appearances trump social grace, even to those who raised her. After the loss of both her inheritance and her adoptive family's support, work as a governess seems to be Anna's only path forward... until she meets a man who is completely unattainable, and she feels seen and accepted for the first time.

Aspiring politician William Thaxton had no intention of falling in love with a governess. But from his first embarrassing encounter with Anna, he knew she was exceptional. As William gets to know Anna better, he can't help falling in love with her, despite the infuriating stumbling block that her social status presents. As they navigate intolerance, cruelty, and William's own ambitions, William and Anna must prove that love knows no boundaries and that the heart doesn't play by Society's rules.

Of Jasmine and Roses is available at Deseret Book or online retailers.

More in Victorians at the Beach

Of Fossils and Follies by Sienna Peake

Will an unexpected summer yield more than one discovery?

Ever since she was a young girl studying geology with her father, Opal Martin has longed for the chance to visit Lyme Regis and dig for discoveries of her own. When a high-stakes contest partners her with the stiff and grumpy Mr. Harris, Opal hardly expects to find love along her quest for fossils.

Nigel Harris has had to work his way up from humble origins to become an assistant to the famous geologist, Gideon Buckston. The last thing he needs is a pampered lady tagging along on his summer explorations. But when his chance to join a prestigious expedition is on the line, he finds the ever-enthusiastic Miss Martin to be just the partner he needs.

Amidst Ruins and Remembrances by Amy Newbold

Ten years have passed since Eloise Deighton's first love, Griffith Hastings, broke her heart. When Griffith unexpectedly returns to the Whitby shore, a tide of memories erodes Eloise's resolve to remain unattached. Now a widower with a six-year-old daughter, Griffith aims to win Eloise back. Even as her feelings for him grow, she fears he will abandon her once again. They must decide if their rekindled attraction is strong enough to overcome the past and give them a second chance at love.

Of Sea and Sorrow by Heloise C. Kensington

Edith Linton sets aside her dreams and concerns for the future and travels to Weymouth, England in the company of her mother and her ailing brother. Seeking to bring better medical practices learned in the Crimea to the residents of the seaside town, Dr. Henry Forester is frustrated by the negative reactions, especially those of his new patient's sister. Edith and Henry must learn to see past their differences before the hope for a happy future is lost.

Of Shells and Serendipity by Karen M. Edwards

A chance encounter blossoms into romance

Elspeth "Elsie" Abercrombie is a dutiful daughter—to a point. Although her mother tries to persuade her to marry, Elsie prefers to study marine biology. Dr. Magnus MacPherson, a former soldier, arrives to teach about battle wounds at the St. Andrews University Medical School for summer term. Magnus originally planned to return home to the Isle of Skye to establish a sanatorium until a sea change happens: a chance encounter with Miss Abercrombie and it's love at first sight. Can Elsie and Magnus reconcile their dreams and ambitions and find a love as deep and enduring as the constant sea?